ONE FINAL STEP

A Novel By: Greg Cole

*Coletrain Group * Leland, NC*

GREG COLE

Coletrain Group

9463 Cottonwood Lane

Leland, NC 28451

Contact the author through his website:
www.gregcolebooks.com

To: Dee, You are the song to my soul

Ah, distinctly I remember it was in the bleak December,

And each separate dying ember wrought its ghost upon the floor.

Eagerly I wished the morrow;--vainly I had sought to borrow

From my books surcease of sorrow--sorrow for the lost Lenore--

For the rare and radiant maiden whom the angels name Lenore--

Nameless here for evermore.

~~Excerpt from The Raven

Edgar Allan Poe

ONE FINAL STEP

Prolog

"Welcome to IUPUI's seminar on Embryonic Stem Cell Research. You are in for quite a treat today. We have with us one of the top scientists in the country, if not the world. She is the foremost authority on Embryonic Stem Cell Research and is on the verge of revolutionizing this area of science. She, herself, graduated from right here at IUPUI just a few years ago. It gives me great pleasure to introduce to you, Doctor Leah Stone!"

Leah stepped to the podium to the sound of twenty-four pairs of hands clapping. She thought such an introduction was not necessary for such a small, intimate audience. She smiled openly to her reception. Her palms were clammy and her heart raced. She was about to give her first seminar on Embryonic Stem Cell Research to a class full of promising young students studying in the same field: seventeen young women and seven young men. She, herself, had been in the field only a few years, by research standards; only nine. Finally, the applause died down and she cleared her throat.

"Thank you all for crawling out of bed on a Saturday morning to come and listen to me bore you back to sleep."

A few chuckles were heard.

"In early November of 1998, when human embryonic stem cells were introduced to the world by James Thomson, from the University of Wisconsin-Madison, the possibilities seemed astonishing. Today, ephemeral, blank slate cells that occur at the earliest stages of human development, can be isolated, cultured, and grown in apparently limitless quantities." Leah paused and looked around the room and some of her nervousness eased. "It is not too unrealistic to say that this research has the potential to revolutionize the practice of medicine and improve the quality and length of life through nearly limitless means. There is almost no realm of medicine that might not be touched by this innovation. Stem cells are one of the most fascinating areas of biology today, but like many expanding fields of scientific inquiry, research on stem cells raises scientific questions as rapidly as it generates new discoveries. There is no doubt among biologists that embryonic stem cells have vast potential. There are no other cells that can perform the same biological feats. They can morph into any one of the two-hundred and twenty types of cells and tissues in the human body. Nurtured in their undifferentiated state, they can proliferate endlessly in culture, and provide a vast supply of cells for research and, someday, therapy. And perhaps most importantly of all, they provide our only window to the earliest stages of human development and, after differentiation, access to more specialized cells that could vastly improve our understanding of the onset of cell-based diseases, and perhaps ways to prevent them. Some of the areas..."

Over the next hour and ten minutes, Leah delivered a very in depth perception on the subject matter. She knew the material was somewhat boring to talk about but exciting as hell to participate in. She noticed throughout that a few heads were bobbing as people would catch themselves dozing off and would try to act like they hadn't.

"Ok, class, that brings me to the end of my lecture. What I'd like to do now is open up the floor to questions." Leah spotted a raised hand, "Ok, you, your question?"

"Yes, Doctor, would you please tell me once again where stem cells come from?" a young lady asked.

"Yes. Human embryonic stem cells are derived from fertilized embryos less than a week old. Next question?" She pointed to another raised hand.

"Yes, ma'am. You said these cells could help with diseases. How might embryonic stem cells be used to treat disease?"

"The ability to grow human tissue of all kinds opens the door to treating a range of cell-based diseases and to growing medically important tissues that can be used for transplantation purposes. For example, diseases like juvenile onset diabetes mellitus and Parkinson's disease occur because of defects in one of just a few cells types. By replacing faulty cells with healthy ones it offers hope of lifelong treatment. Similarly, failing hearts and other organs, in theory, could be shored up by injecting healthy cells to replace damaged or diseased cells." She looked around the class. "Next question?"

"Doctor Stone, if stem cell research is so good, why are so many people against it?"

"Excellent question. Simply stated, most people just don't understand it. It becomes a moral question as to the treatment of embryos. In the case of embryonic stem cell research, the end that scientists hope to achieve is the relief of human suffering. That this is a humanitarian and worthy end is not in dispute. The controversy is about the means, namely, the consumption of donated embryos. More particularly, embryonic stem cell research and therapy would use donated embryos that, by virtue of donor instructions, will never enter a uterus. Is it permissible to use those means to that end? Ancient religious texts provide little guidance. The ancients did not understand embryology, did not imagine that scientists might create and nurture what we now understand as embryos in the laboratory. Nor can we get an answer from laboratory experiments. There is no test for whether an embryo is a person. Instead we are left to our own devices, to our own moral reasoning. Our task is to decide how we should act toward an embryo, and whether we should recognize, as we do among adults, distinctions between embryos of various types and in various circumstances. We immediately encounter the question of what beings we should classify as "persons" for purposes of the duty not to kill persons. Next question?"

"Doctor, why doesn't research just use adult stem cells instead?"

"Adult and embryonic stem cells differ in the number and type of differentiated cells types they can become. Embryonic stem cells can become all cell types of the body because they are pluripotent. Adult stem cells are generally limited to differentiating into different cell types of their tissue of origin. In addition, large numbers of embryonic stem cells can be relatively easily grown in culture, while adult stem cells are rare in mature tissues and methods for expanding their numbers in cell culture have not yet been worked out. This is an important distinction, as large numbers of cells are needed for stem cell replacement therapies. Any other questions?"

A hand went up near the back of the room. Leah noticed a young lady with curly shoulder length auburn colored hair. She pointed to her.

"Yes, Doctor Stone, my question is where do the cells come from and then I would like to know if there is a place where someone, like me, can sell or donate eggs for research."

"Many use fertilized embryos from fertility clinics. Sometimes, couples who are trying to have a baby create several fertilized embryos and don't implant them all. They may donate the ones that are left over to science. As far as the second part to your question, science has recently started allowing healthy women to donate eggs to specialized clinics for the specific purpose of scientific research, much in the same way men donate sperm, blood donors donate blood, and organ donors donate their organs. There is such a clinic available in the city." Leah spoke to the entire class, "If anybody is interested in this process, less the men in the class," she said tongue-in-cheek to received chuckles, "see me after the seminar and I will be happy to give you the information."

A few more questions were asked. Leah had answers for all. Four girls approached her after the seminar for information about the clinic. Leah was happy to provide them with pamphlets and information. The meeting lasted longer than she had anticipated, though, which frustrated her a bit. After all, it was Saturday and she wanted to be home with her husband, Max, and her family. Three hours after she arrived, she was finally able to go home.

Chapter 1

Max Stone jolted awake. With lightning reflexes, he reached for his pistol by the bed. His breathing and his pulse were in a race. For a moment, he thought his heart would pound right through his rib cage. Perspiration beaded on his brow. The nightmares he had been having for the past few nights tore at the very root of his soul. Gone was his steadfast composure. Every sound startled him. Every movement grabbed his attention. This had replaced the norm. The culprit this time was Mario, the family cat.

"Stupid cat," he said to himself as he replaced his head on his pillow.

Mario was sleek, pure black with yellow eyes. He was silent, rarely making any noise. He often made his way to the bed sometime during the night to curl up at the feet of Max and Leah. Tonight he chose 3:15 a.m.

Max's breathing and heartbeat returned to normal. Mario instinctively crept up to the big man's side, licked his hand, and stretched out along him as if to say *"Sorry Max."*

"It's o.k. buddy," Max said quietly as his caressed the cat. He knew this was a nightly ritual, but tonight he was in the middle of one of those disturbing dreams.

He looked over at his wife, Leah. She looked so peaceful lying there. For three nights now, he had kept a secret from her and as a rule, they kept no secrets. His work, however, was a different story. She rarely asked him about it. She simply had no interest unless it involved forensics. He was fine with that because he had no interest in her profession either; Geneticist, whatever the hell that was. So, he spared her from boring details of cases he was involved in and of gruesome things he was forced to see. Hell, he himself found it a little boring at times and very disturbing at others, but it was his life's work and he enjoyed it. He felt detective work chose him, he didn't choose it, and he was damn good at it.

Still, how could he tell her that her life was in danger? Should he tell her? No, he rationalized. The real question was why. Why was her life in danger? What was someone trying prove? These were the questions that had burdened him since the phone call that came three days ago. He played the call in his mind again as he attempted to go back to sleep.

"Max Stone speaking," he said.

"Detective, Max Stone?" A strange voice questioned.

"Yes. How can I help you?"

"Congratulations on your recent award."

Max had recently been awarded "Man of the Year" by Mayor Peterson for heroism "above and beyond the call of duty" for his role in bringing a child killer to justice. He had taken a bullet in his left side during a shoot-out, but nothing serious. The city of Indianapolis, in all its glory, felt it necessary to plaster Max's face all over the newspapers and television to show the world their resident "tough cop." He wished they hadn't publicized it. Just last week, the latest edition of *Indianapolis Monthly* had run a cover story on the heralded detective. This was more exposure than Max wanted or needed. He preferred a low-profile.

"Mr. Stone?" the voice interrupted his thoughts.

"Yeah, I'm still here. Uh, thanks for your support. Who is this?" Max asked.

"Who I am is not important. What I am is."

"I'm listening. Go on."

"I've been watching you, Mr. Stone. I've been keeping track of you."

He was getting that edgy feeling in the pit of his stomach. His senses were kicking in and he knew something was about to ruin his day.

"Really," Max said with sarcasm. "And why is that?"

"Call it a hobby, Mr. Stone."

Max was getting annoyed. "I'm listening. What do you want?"

"Total destruction, Mr. Stone," the voice paused. "I intend to prove that you are not the detective or the man the IPD, and the citizens of Indianapolis think you are. I

9

intend to tarnish the image your beautiful wife has of you. I intend to bring you down so low, Mr. Stone, that your very kids will be disgraced to call you daddy. That's what I want!"

"You sick bastard. Is this some kind of joke?" Max's temper was flaring. "Did I bust your ass before?"

"No, Mr. Stone. You and I have never had the pleasure of meeting, but we will."

"And why is that? Are you itching to be the next one to stare down the barrel of Raven?"

Raven was the affectionate name he had for his pistol. It was a 357-Magnum revolver, the choice of his hero, Dirty Harry. He just loved the way Clint Eastwood portrayed the take-no-shit attitude of the famous cop. Max had the same attitude when provoked. Like Dirty Harry, Max, too, had a famous saying when it came to his pistol; "Quote the Raven, nevermore."

"Come, come, now Mr. Stone." He kept his composure. "Aren't we an angry person?"

"Listen, you bastard, I don't know who you are but I will track you down. When I find you I will stick the end of my gun up your ass and pull the trigger."

The voice let out a chuckle. "Mr. Stone, you don't have to come looking for me. I will come for you when the time is right. How much more fair can I be than that?"

"Name the place and time. I will be waiting for you." "Eager aren't we, Mr. Stone? Don't you even want to know why Mr. Stone?" the voice calmly said.

Max stood on the corner of the busy intersection. His cell phone was glued to his ear as he listened. People watched as he moved around like a lunatic. They walked around to avoid him.

"Mr. Stone, my interest lies with your wife."

"Leah?" Max questioned. "What do you want with my wife?"

"You see, Mr. Stone, as I said, I intend to take you down and show the community that so dearly loves you, that even the great Max Stone couldn't protect his own wife. Your wife will die."

Chapter 2

The sound of the alarm clock warned Max it was time to get up. It was the first sound he remembered hearing since Mario startled him awake. Funny, he didn't remember dozing back to sleep.

He reached over to silence the wailing alarm and noticed the clock read 6:00 a.m.

Leah stirred slightly as if she were looking for him in her sleep. Max turned on his side, as usual, and wrapped his left arm around her body. She let out a slight moan of approval and scooted back against him. His thoughts returned to the mysterious phone call he had received three days ago. It haunted him. What about the kids? God, some sick bastard wouldn't think about hurting their kids, would he? They had two kids; Laura, who was the oldest at sixteen, and Connor, who was twelve. He could never forgive himself if anything ever happened to his family.

The alarm blared again, telling him the nine-minute

snooze had expired. Leah stirred once again and his thoughts returned to her. His desire to have her this morning was growing and she seemed willing.

Suddenly, his cell phone rang. Max thought for a moment to ignore it but, at this hour, it was likely important.

"I'm sorry honey, I have to answer this," he said to his waiting wife.

She showed her disproval but understood.

"Hello, Max Stone. This better be important."

"Max, sorry to bother you this early buddy," the voice said. It was John Thompson, Max's partner and life-long friend.

"What's up, Tank."

Tank was the nickname Max had given his partner long before they ever dreamed of being detectives. John was a burly man, standing over six-foot tall and weighed somewhere in the neighborhood of two-hundred and seventy pounds. He was big as a grizzly bear, but gentle, like Max, unless you gave him cause.

"Max, there's been a murder. Meet me at the entrance to Eagle Creek Park right away."

"Right away?" Max questioned with reluctance.

"Yes!" Tank paused, "And, uh....Max?"

"Huh?"

"Tell Leah she'll have to wait until later to get her some of 'Ol Stoney." He laughed at his own joke. "See you in a few!" He hung up without giving Max a chance to say something smart-assed back.

Tank always seemed to know what Max was up to. They were life-long friends. They were born eight days apart and grew up together in the old neighborhood.

Max turned to Leah. "Sorry, honey, I have to go."

Leah frowned and allowed her playful side to show. "But sweetheart," she pouted. She knew he had to go but she couldn't resist the temptation to make him suffer a little.

He rushed to throw clothes on and leaned to kiss her. "I'll call you later, baby."

He put his revolver into his shoulder holster, raced down the stairs, grabbed his jacket, and was quickly out the door.

The early morning sky was streaked with shades of red and pink with a background of beige-blue, announcing the morning sun would peak above the horizon soon. He could see his breath in the crisp fall air. He climbed in his inferno-orange Camaro and made his way toward Eagle Creek Park. It was on the northwest side of the city. From home, it would take him a good thirty minutes. He popped in a C.D. of some old Sonny Boy Williamson blues and made his way toward the park.

A glance at his watch told him it was 7:25 a.m. when he arrived at the north entrance. Eagle Creek was the largest park in the city. When a person was looking for a day to relax, it was the place to go. Once there, it was easy to forget that you were only twenty minutes from downtown of the twelfth largest city in the United States. The sun was low, slowly climbing above the horizon. The trees had shed their foliage in preparation of the approaching winter months. Their crooked, dark branches made for an eerie sight in the pre-dawn sunlight.

John was sitting in his car at the entrance to the park. Max parked his car and stepped out into the chilly air, clutching his jacket as he did so. He slid in the passenger side of John's car.

"Hell of a way to start a Friday," Max said as he shut the door. John smiled and put the car in drive.

They made their way down Eagle Creek Drive into the park, talking as they drove.

"What took you so long?" John asked.

"Jesus Christ, I got here as fast as I could."

"You had to introduce Leah to 'Ol Stoney before you left didn't you."

"As a matter of fact I did not get a chance to, smart ass," Max joked. "You interrupted me."

"Hey, you're welcome," John chuckled. "You know, you keep that pace up and Leah's going to kill you." He smiled over at his friend. "I'm just looking out for you, buddy."

"You wish! You're just jealous because Shawn's only given it to you once so you have to practice the art of sacofricosis."

"No, twice now," he boasted, "I hit a homerun last night."

"Well, at least one of us got lucky," Max chuckled.

Shawn was John's new girlfriend. She was a good woman with an even temper. She made John happy and that was what was important. Max, Leah, and John always hung out together, and it was great he found a girlfriend so he didn't feel like a third wheel.

"Ouch, you cut me so deep," John chuckled. "Oh, Shawn did say to tell you hi, and to keep it in your pants."

"Thanks a lot! I was in such a hurry I didn't even get my morning coffee, although I see you got some."

"No problem, honey." John playfully blew a kiss at Max as he handed him a steaming cup. "I picked you up a cup at the Big Foot."

"Oh, you're so good to me. Better watch it, you'll make Leah jealous."

"Hey, I'm counting on it."

Soon, the joking stopped as the two detectives tried to set their minds to the task as hand.

"Have you been to the murder scene yet, Tank?" Max asked as he sipped his coffee.

"No. I got the call just before I called you. The only details are that the victim is a young female. She
Is probably nineteen or in her early twenties."

"Raped?"

"Possibly. Her hands and feet were bound, her mouth gagged. Oh, and one more thing," his expression changed in an instant, "she was sliced up and down her abdomen."

"She was cut up? That doesn't sound like a sex crime."

"That's what I've been told. What do you think, ritual killing?"

"It could be, but here?"

The two made their way past the bird sanctuary and parked the car near Coffer Dam. Three squad cars were parked nearby, along with a large white van with bold black letters that read, County Coroner. Three police officers were guarding the area near the entrance to a path that made its way along the dam. One officer, Corporal Willis was questioning an obvious jogger. Peggy Meece, from the Coroner's investigative team was standing beside the van.

She was a sweet girl with a petite frame. Max estimated she was in her mid to late twenties. Her hair was short, reddish-blond, about shoulder length. Her tanned skin highlighted the freckles that traced under her green eyes. When Max first met her, he took an instant liking to her. Whatever the situation, her bubbly and perky personality would always lighten the mood. Working at the Coroner's office didn't fit Peggy at all. She had been with the office only a short time and the gore had yet to catch up with her. She had worked with Max and John a couple of times and looked to them, sort-of, like big brothers.

Max and John stepped out of the car and were greeted by her.

"Good morning gentlemen," she acknowledged both detectives. "How are you two?"

Max was the first to answer. "I got to be honest with you, Peggy. I've have better starts to my day, especially a Friday morning." Max nodded towards the man Corporal

Willis was interviewing. "I take it that man discovered the body?"

"Yeah, he's pretty shook up," she said sadly.

"Did he see anything?" John asked.

"I don't know."

"Where is the crime scene?" Max asked.

"Just down that path about a hundred yards." She pointed with her gloved hand.

"Well, let's get this over with, Tank. Peggy, you know the routine. Let's go."

Peggy grabbed Max by the arm. "Max?"

He looked at her with puzzlement. Something was troubling her. Her bright-green eyes turned dull as they watered.

"I have to tell you, Max, it's not a pretty sight down there. It's clear she died a horrific death. I don't know if I can go back."

Max had seen plenty in all his years of homicide work. He was equally sure a person in Peggy's profession had seen plenty too, but not her; not this early into her career. Why did this one bother her so much? He wasn't sure he really wanted to know.

"Should we call in another investigator from your office?"

She swallowed hard. "No, I will be ok."

"Then, shall we," he said, motioning once again.

The three made their way to the gravel pathway that provided access along the entire length of the dam. It was built primarily for birdwatcher and it provided a good vantage point to scan the northern end of the reservoir.

Today, its beautiful view was tarnished with blood stains. They crossed the hundred yards to the crime scene. Two additional officers were there, along with a forensic science specialist. At the far end of the dam were two additional investigators, who were combing the area nearby.

"Son-of-a-bitch!" Tank said when he saw the body. "My mind wasn't prepared for this. Who would do something like this?"

He looked toward Peggy and apologized for his language.

"I warned you two," she said.

"Yes, you warned us, Peggy," Max said. "But I don't think words could really describe this."

Peggy squatted down and opened the investigative kit she was carrying. She produced two sets of surgical gloves and handed them to the detectives. Then she stood and dropped her head slightly, trying not to take in more than she absolutely had to.

They thanked her and slid their hands into the latex gloves.

"Well, my friend," Max said to his partner, "looks like it's going to be a long day."

Tank agreed.

Their good friend, Terry Green, a forensic specialist, approached them. He was a thirty-year veteran of the IPD and considered among the best of the best when it came to forensic science. His aging body, now slowing, was packing a few extra pounds on his six-foot frame. His brown eyes narrowed, revealing crow's feet, as he smiled at them.

"Good morning Max, John," he said in his distinguished voice, nodding to each as he addressed them.

"Yeah, yeah," the two detectives said in unison. They smiled back and shook his hand.

"What's the story, Terry?" Max asked.

"Not a pretty scene at all; worst I've seen in quite some time." He pondered as he continued, "As near as we can tell, it happened sometime during the night."

"Anybody hear anything?" Tank asked.

"Corporal Willis is interviewing a jogger that discovered the body. That's all we have so far."

"Yeah, we saw them talking," Max said. "Any evidence?"

"Some, but you should know I think we are dealing with a professional."

Max was puzzled.

"Max," he said soberly. "There was one piece of evidence we were supposed to find."

He produced a clear plastic evidence bag. Contained inside was a smaller baggie that held a note.

"We found it safety-pinned to her navel. It was meant to be found."

"What's it say?"

"We need these more than you."

"Need what?" Max asked.

"We aren't sure yet, we'll learn more when they do the autopsy. From the looks of the cuts on her abdomen, and the placement of the note, I would guess reproductive organs."

Peggy excused herself.

"Poor girl," Max said.

"We've also recovered her clothing and her purse. They were near her body."

"Do you know the victim's name?" Max asked.

"Her name was Misty Lawrence, according to her IUPUI student I.D. and her driver's license. We found them in her purse. Here is the rest of the information you will need." He handed Max a piece of paper.

Max looked at the print. It had the usual information; name, address, date of birth, etc.

"Her parents been notified?"

"Yes, of course."

"Any other evidence?" Max asked as he shoved the piece of paper into his pocket.

"We haven't found any prints nor do we really expect to. The killer was thorough. Of course, it's early. We did find some skin samples under her nails among the dirt," he said, adding hope. "We will have that analyzed as quickly as we can. No other D.N.A. has been found. You know the usual routine. Hopefully we'll find something more substantial. We have collected some hair and blood samples, but right now it's difficult to determine if they belong to her or someone else."

"Was she raped?"

"We don't believe so. When you're done here I'll have the county coroner's office take her to the morgue and we'll have her examined."

"Well," Max turned to Tank, "let's finish up and let Terry get back to his work."

John agreed.

"Thanks, Terry," Max said. "We'll check in with you at the office later today."

They said their goodbyes and the detectives went back to work.

The body lay on the side of the embankment just off the gravel path on the reservoir side. Her head was closest to the path and her feet were near the water's edge. She was positioned on her back. Her hands were tied above her head and were anchored to the ground. Her legs were spread and her feet were bound the same as her hands. Her jeans had been cut from her small frame and were strewn to her side. Her shirt was unbuttoned, but left on her body, and her red satin bra was still in place, covering her breasts. The attacker had left her shoes and socks on her as well.

Large, deep, perfectly executed incisions ran from each side of her abdomen down to her vaginal area. They had the precision of a well skilled surgeon. Blood had run down both her sides and caked onto the ground around her. Parts of her intestines had oozed through the cuts and were exposed. Max looked at the young woman's face. "She was absolutely terrified when she died," he said to Tank in a low tone.

John agreed.

Max looked up toward Peggy. Her back was slightly turned to them.

"Peggy?" Max called to her.

She turned.

"Are you ok?"

"Yes, Max," she said as her voice quivered. "I'm just shook up. This girl was so young, nearly as young as I am, and someone cut her up. This was so senseless." Her hands shook and a tear dripped down her cheek. "Then he left her here to bleed to death." She put her hands over her face, turned to walk back to the gravel path, and stood with her back to the scene as the two detectives continued their investigation.

"We better call in another person from the Coroner's office," Max said.

Chapter 3

Leah Stone started her day the way she always did. She awoke to the alarm clock at 7a.m. and rolled over to clutch Max's pillow. She wondered what mess he was into right now. He received a call from his partner, John, and flew out of the house early this morning. It seemed his life was always marred with work interruptions. It was something he had gotten used too long ago. She, on the other hand, was only starting to get used to it, or was it she was just learning to deal with it.

After a few moments, she threw on her robe and made her way to the shower to start her day. After her shower, she leisurely got dressed for work, combed her hair, and put her makeup on. Satisfied with her look, she woke the children for school, and made her way down the stairs to have her morning caffeine. She despised coffee so her drink of choice was Coke. She couldn't start her day without one. She checked the clock and it read 7:43. She had enough time for a bagel and to make some oatmeal for the kids.

Laura and Connor made their way to the table just as she was sitting the steaming bowls of cereal on the table.

"Good morning mom," they said in unison, rubbing the sleep from their eyes.

"Good morning kids."

"Where's dad?" Laura asked.

"He got called away to work, honey."

She poured each a glass of milk then grabbed up her purse and car keys.

"Kids, I'm running late for work. You know the drill. Finish your breakfast, brush your hair and your... "

She was playfully interrupted by Laura. "Teeth and make sure our faces are clean."

"And don't forget our lunch money. Make sure all the lights are out," Connor added.

"And make sure the door is locked and get to the bus stop on time," Laura finished.

Leah didn't need to tell the kids every morning, but she did. They were old enough to know what to do anyway. She kissed them both and made her way to the door, grabbing her jacket as she left.

She used her drive time, like she did each morning, as her personal time. She always listened to her favorite station and the Smiley morning show. Just as she was getting into her car, her favorite song, *The Edge of Glory*, by

Lady Gaga, was coming on the radio. It was going to be a good day.

Leah and Max differed in music choice. She loved top-forty and he was a blues guy. When they were together in the car, there were usually compromises made, but Max won most of the time.

She made her way around the south loop of the city and headed toward downtown to the Indiana University Hospital, where she worked in Biomedical Science Research Center.

Leah had earned her Bachelor of Cytotechnology degree from Indiana University/Purdue University in Indianapolis (IUPUI) in the summer of '98 and continued her education there, earning her PhD in Biogenetics in '04.

She was considered one of the top-ten scientists in the field. She was even a recipient of the Frank Annunzio award, an annual award given to living Americans for improving the world through ingenuity and innovation. It was also intended to provide incentive for continuing research or a specific project.

More specifically, she was enamored in the development of cloning embryonic stem cells for the development of internal organs. This was an unheard of area of technology but Leah had a vision of making this happen. The university appointed her the lead scientist over a team of two others dedicated to this field of study. She thought how wonderful it would be to be able to provide a liver to someone who desperately needed one; and the cellular tissue would be an exact duplicate of the patient's own cell development. Oh, the possibilities! No more worries about the body rejecting the organ that's invading its body. With dedication to this process, she would make it happen. This could even have potential to eliminate the waiting list of people in need of organ transplants. People would no longer be dying while waiting. How wonderful!

She pulled her Eos into the parking lot, drove up to the guard shack, and flashed her credentials. The guard placed his forefinger to the brim of his black hat and let her pass.

Most of the hospital and facility areas were easily accessible. But some, like the Biomedical Research Laboratory, were highly classified.

She pulled into the space marked, *"Leah A. Stone, PhD,"* and made her way to the building. She showed her credentials to another guard and was permitted to enter.

Once inside, she would meet with the other two scientists on her team; Freda Lyle and Douglas Brewer, both PhD's.

Even though Leah was the youngest of the three, and the least tenured, she was the most intelligent of the three by far.

Douglas, or "The Stain," as Leah and Freda liked to call him, was the oldest and nearing retirement. Freda, of course, was in the middle, which was par for her. She was in the middle of just about everything.

The daily routine way typical, whoever got there first would wait for the others to arrive. Then, all three would walk together to the lab. Today, Leah was second. Freda was sipping her morning coffee, waiting.

"Good morning, Freda," Leah said.

"Morning, Leah."

"Douglas is last again, I see."

"Of course, did you expect less?"

"No," Leah chuckled, "not really. He's always the last to arrive and always wants to leave early."

The two chatted a few more minutes until the door to the lobby opened.

"Finally, here he comes," Freda motioned toward the door.

Doctor Douglas Brewer approached the two ladies. He was an average looking man. His eyes were dark walnut and were fronted by the small square-shaped lenses of his glasses. The only hair he had left on his head was a small mustache that was salt and pepper in color. He was in his usual attire; brown dress slacks, light blue button-down shirt, plain tie, and white lab coat unbuttoned down the front. He completed his ensemble with a pocket protector stuffed full of pens.

"Good morning, ladies," he said to them in his mundane tone.

The two women looked at each other with an "oh brother," look on their face and greeted him in a mawkish, playful manner.

"Cute, ladies," he said in a monotone voice.

Leah and Freda were always trying to get under his skin. They found him to be too stuffy. Douglas could best be described as the typical, stiff, boring laboratory scientist.

"Oh lighten up, Douglas," Leah said.

Freda giggled under her breath. She liked to see the two pick at one another. They were polar opposites. Leah was friendly, energetic, playful, and outgoing. Douglas, on the other hand, was an introvert. He was quiet, a strict professional, and, well, damn boring.

He looked down over the top of his glasses, "Are you two ladies ready?" he questioned as he gestured toward the hall with the wave of his arm.

Freda gulped the last drink of her coffee. "Sure. Let's roll, Doc."

Leah rolled her eyes at her, "Me too."

Leah and Freda followed, making faces at him behind his back.

Chapter 4

Max and John arrived at headquarters around 10:00 a.m. They were greeted, upon entering the building, by the office secretary, Helen Weddel.

"Hey, guys," she said.

She was a sweet grandma type woman, retirement age, Max guessed. She was thin with a short, tight curled perm. Her clothing was conservative, usually slacks, and very little make up.

"Good morning, Helen," Max said as he browsed through his messages in his mail box.

"The captain left word he wanted to see you two as soon as you came in." She could see the puzzlement in their eyes and added, "Said he wanted a briefing about the homicide you were investigating from this morning. It's all I know."

The two detectives thanked Helen, and proceeded to the coffee pot.

"Better get a bracer," Max said, reaching for the coffee.

"I'm with you, buddy."

The two poured their steaming hot brew, each in their own special coffee mug. Max, with his ceramic mug that proclaimed him *"World's Best Husband,"* compliments of his wife, and John, with his personalized ceramic mug that read, *"Detective Tank Thompson."*

With coffee in hand, they proceeded to the boss's office, arriving at a wooden door bearing the name "Captain Robert L. Lee."

Max knocked on the slightly ajar door and pushed it open.

"Come in boys and have a seat," the Captain said.

They entered and approached burgundy-colored chairs. The leather creaked as they sat. Behind the cherry wood desk sat Captain Lee, a Sherman Potter look-alike, according to most.

"You wanted to see us, Captain?" Max asked.

"Yes. I heard you boys had quite a morning."

"Yeah, it wasn't pretty."

"That's what I heard. Give me the details."

For the next several minutes the three men talked. Details were given about what Max and John had witnessed. With each gruesome detail, the Captain grimaced a bit. Even with all his years of police work and, after seeing it all, it still bothered him to hear of such brutality. He just couldn't understand the evils of people. What made people do the things they did? Why? Why?

Why? Always questions, seldom answers. This is one part of the job he would not miss when he retired.

"Any leads to go on?" the Captain asked.

Max paused and thought for a moment. "Well, there was a jogger who discovered the body, but didn't see anything," Max said. "Apparently he lives in a housing edition nearby and jogs that trail regularly."

The three sat in silence for what seemed like an hour. Max began to hear his own heartbeat in his eardrums as his thoughts drifted. It started silently at first but grew louder with each ticking second of the clock.

Senseless murder was horrible enough, but why in the hell would someone slice up a beautiful young woman? Was it motivated by rape? Not likely this time, but they hadn't heard back from the Coroner's office. But if it was, why would they run a surgical knife down both sides of the abdomen? She had also been bleeding from her vagina. Was it an abortion gone terribly wrong? Her boyfriend, perhaps, making sure she didn't give birth? That could be a possible motivation for a murder, Max reasoned. And, what the hell was with the note? It read, *"We need these more than you do."* These what? What did that mean? What was the killer trying to say? For that matter, why her? What the hell did she do to the killer? Anything? She sure didn't deserve to die, whatever it was. What were the killer's motives?

"Max," John said sharply while shaking the big man.

Max shook his head to clear the cobwebs. He looked at his partner and then the captain, who had a furrow in his brow.

"Sorry about that, captain," he finally said. "I was deep in thought."

"I understand, Max. I've come to expect that from you. The truth is you do your best work when you've had time to collect your thoughts. I know that about you." The Captain paused to collect his own thoughts. "Hell, I was the same way when I was your age."

"If you ask me, he goes off the deep end every once in a while," John said. "I think, sometimes, he's going to blow a circuit. The man's stressed." He chuckled.

"Captain, I was thinking," Max said while straightening himself in the chair. "That note we found on the victim?" he said questioningly. The captain nodded as if he was saying, go on. "Don't you think that is an indication the killer will likely do this again?"

"Logical," he agreed. "Any other clues to go on?"

"No, we're still waiting on Terry Green from forensics and Peggy Meece from the Coroner's office to get back with us. We're hoping something will turn up there that we can use. All we know for sure is that her name was Misty Lawrence, age twenty-one, and a college student.

"You two want a refill on your cups?" the captain asked as he helped himself to the pot of fresh coffee he had in his office.

"No thanks," John said, covering his mug with his hand.

Max took the last gulp from his mug, "Sure, Captain. I can use one."

Max thanked him as the Captain filled his cup. The steam rose, bringing the fresh smell of coffee to his nostrils.

"Sugar?" the captain motioned to the bowl.

"No. Thank you. You know I take my coffee black, Captain."

A wry smile crept across Captain Lee's face as he looked at his favorite detective. "I guess there's no need to offer cream then?" He chuckled.

Max shook his head as he sipped.

"Well, suit yourself," he said as he doctored his coffee with a little cream and two spoonsful of sugar.

Max watched his hand as he stirred. The sound of the spoon clanking against the ceramic mug was something he didn't like the sound of. To him, it sounded like chains on a ghost. He didn't know why, it just was.

The three were still discussing the case when Max's cell phone rang. "It's Leah," Max said without looking at the caller I.D. "She has her own special ring."

"Now, isn't that sweet," John joked with his friend.

Captain Lee chuckled.

"Sorry, captain."

"Nonsense. Aren't you going to answer it?"

"Is it ok with you?"

"Answer the poor girl. It could be important. Oh, and tell the Mrs. I said hello."

As soon as Max answered, John began making kissing noises. The captain motioned at him to stop but had no luck. He knew these two were best friends and the best damn detectives he had. Their chemistry meshed perfectly. Both had a comical side and a serious side and they were always on the same page.

"Tank, Leah says to quit making passes at me before she gets jealous," Max said. "She also wants to know if you and Shawn are still joining us for dinner tonight at Sanqunetti's."

Shawn was John's new girlfriend of about a month. They met at O'Rourke's, a popular martini bar on the northeast side of the city. The three were out that night for a few drinks. The two men were drinking Red Stag bourbon, with beer chasers, and Leah was enjoying her usual chocolate martini. She was joking with them, trying to get them to try a trendy martini, affectionately called, *"Green Silk Panties"* when the fight broke out.

Shawn was actually there shooting pool with a date. They got into an argument over something; about what, they didn't know. Shawn's date came up to John and accused him of flirting with her and asked him to step outside to settle it like men. John chuckled at him and told him to go sit down before he got hurt. This made the man furious and he challenged John again, accusing him of being afraid. Shawn was begging her boyfriend to stop, but he wouldn't listen to her. He turned and shoved her to the floor, which pissed John off.

He unfolded his bear-like frame from the chair and stood inches from the man. When he saw how big John actually was, his courage fled. He turned to his girlfriend, who was picking herself up off the floor, grabbed her arm, and demanded they leave immediately. She pulled away and promptly told him to go to hell. He started to say something else to her but decided not to when John walked up behind him and whispered something into his ear. She thanked him for helping her and started to walk away. John playfully told her she could at least have a drink with him and his friends. He sensed her hesitation, so he smiled at her, showed her his badge, and, in only a way that John A. Thompson could do, told her she was under arrest. He sentenced her to have a drink with him. The rest was history. As it turned out, the argument was over how she had noticed John's wavy black hair and chiseled good looks. He never told what he whispered in the man's ear.

"Yes, Shawn and I are looking forward to it," John said.

Max confirmed the date and went on to other business. Their conversation lasted a few minutes longer, and he hung up the phone.

"Sorry about that, Captain," Max apologized.

"No problem, son," he said, holding up his right hand as if to say stop.

Suddenly there was a knock on the door. It was Helen.

"I'm terribly sorry, Captain," she said. "Peggy Meece from the county Coroner's office is here to see Max and John."

Both detectives shot up from their seats as if they were stuck in the ass with a straight pin. They looked at the Captain for permission to be dismissed.

"Go. Go do your job," he said as he gestured to scoot them out the door.

Chapter 5

Peggy Meece was sitting at Max's desk. She stood as the two detectives approached her. Max could tell she had been crying. Her eyes were puffy and dark circles had formed.

Max opened his arms and gave her a comforting hug. "How ya doing Peggy?"

"Her female parts are missing!" she forced, her voice trembling as she pushed away from him.

"I was afraid of that," Max said to his partner.

Shock was on her face. "The bastard took her ovaries and fallopian tubes. Why?"

"I don't know, Peggy, but we will find out."

"That explains the incisions," Tank said somberly.

Max asked Peggy to sit at his desk as John retrieved some water from the cooler and handed it to her.

"Peggy, one possible theory we have is the perpetrator could be a boyfriend. Perhaps she was carrying an unwanted child or something. Was she pregnant?"

"No, she wasn't pregnant."

"One theory down," John said.

"Not necessarily," Max corrected. "Maybe she was unfaithful and the boyfriend went nuts."

"Well, it's possible, but we don't even know if she had a boyfriend."

"True," Max said as he reached for the coffee pot.

Max poured himself a cup. He usually only had two or three cups in the morning and then turned his tastes to Coke or juice, but today just seemed like a coffee kind of day.

He sat the pot down just in time to see Terry Green.

"Max!" he said, waving a folder as he approached.

"Hello again, Terry," Max said with an extended hand.

"I figured you would want this right away," he said as he returned the hand shake.

"Yes, but how the hell did you get it that quick?"

"Because I'm good. I knew you would want this quick, fast, and in a hurry," he said, using one of Max's old lines.

"You remember Peggy Meece?"

"Yes," he said as he acknowledged her.

"I appreciate it, Terry. Tell me what you got. Was she raped?"

"Well, we don't know for sure. There was semen found, and some vaginal bruising, but we can't be sure if that was the cause or the motive. Obviously, with her vagina being abused the way it was," he turned and apologized to Peggy for the visuals, "we can't be sure if the intercourse was a prior consensual act or a motive of the murder itself. I do know she wasn't pregnant."

"Yeah, we've been advised of that but the semen might help rejuvenate one of our theories."

"What theory is that?"

"We were acting on the theory that she had a boyfriend and he killed her as an abortion attempt, but, there was no pregnancy. Then, we moved to the theory that she was unfaithful so her boyfriend killed her, taking her reproductive organs. Now, with the presence of semen, that theory could still be valid."

John added, "It might explain the incisions, and possibly the note. With the confirmation that her reproductive organs were gone it would, of course, prevent her from getting pregnant, providing she would've survived."

Max's thoughts returned to the note. He couldn't get the image out of his head. It seared his brain. What did the note mean? And what was the significance of pinning it to her belly button? The words played in his head like a song he couldn't shake: *"We need these more than she does."* Who needs a woman's reproductive organs worse than she does? What the hell would someone do with them? Why was this woman punished? There had to be a link there somewhere. Was she chosen at random? If so, then why? Max had many questions and very few answers.

"Terry?" John asked, "Was there anything in her blood?"

"Nothing illegal, if that's what you mean. Her blood alcohol level indicated she had a couple of drinks but not much."

"Was there any bruising, besides the obvious?" Max asked.

"I'm not going to lie to you, Max. This woman was tortured. We found bruising around her wrists, of course, from the ropes. We also found bruising on her left cheek where she had been hit. Her legs were scratched up and bruised, I'm guessing, at least partially from the ground. And, of course, there's her abdomen and vaginal area."

"Max, if you guys don't need me for anything else, I'd like to go. This talk gets to me."

"Sure, Peggy, I understand. If I need more, I'll call you."

Peggy rose from her seat, thanked the gentlemen, and started to leave. She took a few steps, and turned to faced them. "You know, I see dead people almost every day. It always gets to me at least a little. But, when they have to die for no reason..." She stopped, turned, and left.

"This one is really getting to her," John said.

"I would expect no less, but we've got to let her work it
out in her way," Max said. "Terry, do you have anything else for us?"

"So far, no," he said as shook his head. "It's clear the killer used gloves, probably surgical. We haven't found any prints. Also, money was not an issue. We found $118 and some change on her. We're still evaluating the hair and skin samples. Maybe we'll get lucky. If we find anything else, I'll let you know." He glanced at his clipboard. "Also, I did give you her personal information, didn't I?"

Max's desk phone rang.

"Tank, will you grab that for me and take a message?"

"Sure."

"Yes, I have it and I've already contacted her parents. John and I are going to talk with them this afternoon. As you can imagine, they were devastated, but I explained how important it was to talk to us as soon as possible."

"Thanks! We'll get right on it!" John said as he hung up the phone. He looked up from the desk with eyes wide. "Max, they found her car!"

Chapter 6

"Tell me the details?" Max asked as soon as they got to the car.

"The car was reported as abandoned just a little while ago by management at the Rathskeller."

In an attempt to be responsible, cars were often left at bars by patrons who had been drinking. Most restaurants would simply allow the car to sit in the parking lot until the offender, once sober, returned to pick up the car. Some, however, would have the vehicle towed, at the owner's expense, of course. What assholes, Max thought.

"The police were sent out, they ran the plates, and discovered the car belonged to Misty Lawrence. So, they called us."

"Please tell me they did not move the car."

"The car is still there, but it has been loaded."

"Why in the hell did they touch the fucking car?"

"They said the flat-bed had it loaded before the police ran the plates. At least they stopped when they found out."

"Well, thank God for that, at least. Call her parents and tell them we will have to push back our meeting."

While John was calling the parents, Max was busy on the phone calling Terry Green to send out a forensics team to examine the car.

Off to the West, the sky had turned a battleship gray, making the afternoon sky look as if it were dusk. Funny how Indiana weather can change so much in so little time. All day it had been in the 40's, which was good for late-November. The forecast was calling for a cold front to push through from the north, dropping the temperature down to around freezing and with it, a cold rain.

They pulled into the drive-thru at a McDonald's for a sandwich on the go. Max wasn't really into fast food. His taste in cuisine was a little more sophisticated. He enjoyed good home-cooked meals with his family, or dining out somewhere nice with his wife and friends and a good bottle of wine or a cold beer. However, it was after lunch and he hadn't had a thing to eat all day so he gave in to his growling stomach.

He took a bite from his sandwich and wondered if his wife would be bitching at him for eating garbage. He tried to eat healthier, even choosing to frequent deli-style restaurants when he could but sometimes a man just needed some roughage. Sure, he was eating McDonald's now, but tonight it would be wood-smoked rack of lamb and a salad at Sanqunetti's with his wife and friends. They would have a great meal and share some great laughs while sharing a few drinks.

They arrived at the Rathskeller, a trendy downtown German restaurant and bar, at 2:15 p.m. Max, himself, had eaten there before and found the food to be wonderfully authentic. He liked to go there in the summer to listen to live music in the outdoor beer garden and have a few brews. Max was partial to German wheat and micro-brewed beers. He could find both there. His favorite: Paulaner. Great beer and live music, especially blues; what more could one ask for.

The red Cavalier belonging to Misty Lawrence was strapped down to a flat-bed hauler when the detectives arrived. A single uniformed cop was standing guard as a half-dozen or so bystanders gawked to try to find out what was going on.

John pulled into an empty spot by the front door and they entered the restaurant.

"Oh, excuse me sir," a man muttered, without eye contact, as he shuffled past the two detectives and left.

"Damn, do we look that intimidating?" Max asked.

"Well, you do look kind of sexy all dressed in black like that and all," John joked.

"Tell me," Max paused for a moment, "why do people always seem afraid of the police? They always have that, I'm not doing anything wrong, look on their faces."

"Maybe you're just scary, my friend."

Max flipped his buddy off.

A big grin crossed John's face. "You better put that away. I'll break that thing off and Leah will be mad at both of us."

Max yanked his hand down and stuffed it in his pocket as if he were afraid. They both had a good laugh.

They approached the bar and were greeted warmly by a cute brunette who appeared to be in her late 20's. She was wearing a silky blue shirt that was cut just low enough to show the top of her ample breasts. Her black slacks cinched in around her slim waist to accent her hips and bottom. Her hair was shoulder length and curly and she went heavy on the make-up. Her eyes were hazel and sparkled, and her lips were adorned with bright red lipstick.

"Good afternoon, gentlemen," her angelic voice greeted, "how may I serve you?"

"Hello," Max replied as he flashed his badge, "I'm Detective Max Stone and this," he motioned to his partner, who was now showing his badge, "is Detective John Thompson."

"It's nice to meet you, gentlemen. I was told two detectives were coming in to see me today but they didn't tell me you were strapping handsome hunks." She flirted as she flashed a brilliant smile that revealed perfectly straight, white teeth.

Max was a bit amused by her actions. He always found it humorous to see a woman use her sexuality for advancement. She was obviously a pro at flirting with men and probably used to getting her way. Although Max enjoyed the attention, in his eyes, most women like that were damaged goods. Sure they were fun to flirt with and, if unattached, to have fun with, but that's about it. On the other hand, what man didn't like the attention of a beautiful woman?

"Well, thank you, uh..., Sorry, I didn't get your name," Max said.

"My name is Celeste Schneider, sweetie," she said as she leaned across the bar, allowing a good view down her shirt. They noticed.

Max couldn't control his wondering eyes as he stole a quick glance at her spilling breasts, hoping he would not get caught. John, however, more or less stared.

"See anything you like, sugar?" She winked at John.

His face turned red as he jerked his eyes away. "I, uh, I'm very sorry, but they were right there on display."

"It's ok, honey," she said as she giggled in her flirty voice. "I don't mind."

Max was getting a little angry. "Can we just get to why we are here?"

"Yes, sorry Max," John apologized.

"Yes sir, I'm sorry too," Celeste said.

"Now, Miss Schneider, Do you know why we are here?"

"Please call me Celeste."

"Ok, Celeste. Do you know why we are here?"

"When I was told by the officer outside, guarding that car, that two detectives were coming to see me about an incident last night, I figured it was about that fight between those two men."

"No, Celeste, we aren't here about two men fighting."

"Am I in some sort of trouble?" she asked with concern.

Max ignored her question as he dug a photo from his jacket. "Do you recognize the woman in this picture?"

She studied the photo for a moment. "Yes, she was in here last night with a real sexy man. In fact, he..." she hesitated. "Is he in trouble?"

"He what? It's very important, Celeste. What did he do?"

"Well, he and the girl got in a big fight because she saw us flirting. They started screaming at each other and he pulled her out of the bar by her arm. He came back by himself a couple hours later. I thought they broke up."

"Celeste, tell us what you know," John demanded.

"I don't know what time they got here but I do know he left here around 10 p.m. Then he came back around, oh, I'd say midnight and left at about 1:00 again when we closed."

Max was writing feverously in his notepad.

"Do you know his name?"

"I believe it was Nathan Anderson."

"Do you know where he is now?"

"No."

"Did you know him before last night?"

"No. I swear. Last night was the first time I ever saw him. Did he do something wrong?"

"Let's put it this way, the girl he was with was found dead this morning at Eagle Creek Park."

A look of disbelief swept across her face. "He killed that young lady?"

"That's why we're here; to figure that out."

"Did this man leave with anyone at 1:00 a.m.?"

Celeste's voice cracked and small beads of perspiration formed on her forehead. "Yes, Mr. Stone. Like I said he was sexy. I'm afraid he left here with me."

Chapter 7

"I'm afraid, Miss Schneider, we're going to have to take a recorded statement from you right now," Max said.

Her face expressed concern. "Am I in trouble? Can I have an attorney?"

He ignored the first question and went straight to the second. "You have the right to an attorney, but that will require us to detain you and take you to headquarters for further questioning. Of course, it's your choice."

"Can I have an attorney come here and you record my statement?"

"Sorry," Max said, shaking his head. "If you have nothing to hide, it shouldn't be a problem, should it?"

Her brow furrowed as she thought for a moment. She reluctantly agreed to the recording.

"Good. Why don't you get us each a Coke and meet us over at that table," Max said, pointing to a table off to the side.

Max sent John out to the car to retrieve a digital recorder. If she was innocent of any involvement and she was called upon as a witness, she wouldn't be able to change her story. On the other hand, if the evidence showed she was involved, they would have her statements to combat her lies.

In reality, should it come down to it, there was only a fifty-fifty chance it could actually be used in a court, but she didn't know that. It would be at the judge's discretion. A slick attorney could easily convince a judge the recording was hearsay evidence and violated the defendant's constitutional rights under the confrontation clause. However, if the recording was voluntary, and was stated so, some judges would still allow it.

"Here are your drinks, gentlemen," she said as she sat down, scooted up to the table, intertwined her fingers, and took a deep breath. "I'm ready when you are."

Max turned on the tape recorder. "This is Detective Max Stone along with Detective John Thompson, both of the Indianapolis Police Department. The time is," he looked at his watch, "4:18 p.m. on Friday, November nineteen, two-thousand and ten. We are conducting this interview at the Rathskeller Restaurant in downtown Indianapolis with Miss Celeste Schneider, bartender of the restaurant."

Over the next few minutes, Max conducted preliminary statements leaving nothing out. He made sure she had clearly stated her name, age, address, and so on. He also read her rights to her and stated she was making the statement voluntarily and without duress.

"Ok, Celeste, I need you, in your own words, to tell me exactly everything you know about Misty Lawrence, Nathan Anderson, and what took place at the Rathskeller on Thursday evening, November 18th, 2010."

Celeste cleared her throat, took a drink of her Coke, and began, "Well, I don't know what time Nathan and the girl came into the Rathskeller but I noticed him around 9:45. He had come up to the bar to order drinks. I thought he was kind of cute so, well, I started flirting with him. I figured no harm since I flirt with a lot of men, and sometimes women too. Anyway, Nathan starts flirting back with me. So, I asked him if the woman he was with was his girlfriend. He told me she wasn't and that she was just some girl he was out with as a favor to a buddy. He told me she was boring and no fun to be with. He said he was getting ready to take her home and dump her off and go have some real fun. So, I asked him where he was going for the real fun. He said he didn't know and that it depended on me. I asked him how it depended on me and that's when he asked me out. Well, I thought he was cute, and I was a little horny, so I asked him if would like to come over to my apartment when I got off work and we could have a few drinks and whatever. He accepted and I gave him my address and phone number. I told him I would get off around one and he said he would just meet me here. So, he left here with that woman around 10:00 p.m. That's the last I saw of him until around midnight when he came back without her. After that, we went back to my apartment, he spent the night, and he left around eleven this morning when I got ready for work. I don't know where he went and I haven't heard from him since."

"When the two of you left here last night, did he ride with you, or did he follow you to your apartment?" Max asked.

"He followed me in his car."

"What kind of vehicle does he drive?"

"I don't know. I know it's blue."

Max knew that line of questioning would go nowhere so he changed direction.

"Now, you say Mr. Anderson and Miss Lawrence left together?"

"Yes."

How were they interacting when they left here?"

"Oh, they were in a big argument," she said.

"Do you know why?"

"I'm afraid I do," she said apologetically. "She saw Nathan and me talking and got quite upset."

"Did you talk to her at all?" John asked.

"No, I just saw her across the room when he and I were talking. I could tell she was getting pissed, and when they left she was in a very animated argument with him."

"Describe what you mean?"

She was flapping her arms around and pointing towards me and things. She made quite a scene and I know she was embarrassing him. When they left, he had her by the arm, almost dragging her outside."

"Celeste," Max leaned forward in his chair, "if you saw all this," he paused, "knew all of this, why in the hell did you still agree to meet with him later?"

Celeste showed a little anger, "Detective," she said in a stern voice, "I don't have to discuss morals with you. I have already told you. I'm a flesh and blood woman, I like sex, and I thought he was cute. I really don't care if the man I want to have sex with happens to have a girlfriend. Hell, I've been with lots of men, and even women; some of them married. I just don't give a shit. I'm not looking for a relationship. Besides, he told me she wasn't his girlfriend and that he was only with her for one night as a favor to a friend." Celeste crossed her arms in a defensive posture. The gesture pushed her cleavage up a little more. She took a deep breath, which swelled her ample breast even more as the bra and her shirt strained to hold them in their place. She looked as if she were about to pout as she let a deep breath escape her lungs.

"Ok, Miss Schneider," Max said. "Tell me, then, why, if he was showing hostility towards her, didn't you report this to the police last night?"

"She was hostile towards him as well. Besides that, couples get into arguments in here all the time." Her voice changed to one of a smart-ass. "You may find this hard to believe, but most of the time it's over someone of the opposite sex. Sometimes, even over me. There was no real threat or reason to call the police in my opinion, Mr. Stone." She finished with a definitive nod of the head.

Max gestured for her to calm down. "I understand a lot of people get into disagreements over the opposite sex. I can appreciate that. Why wasn't her car reported when it sat out there all night?"

"Again, detective," she said, "a lot of people come here to drink and have a good time. Some are smarter than others. They leave their car here because they are too drunk to drive and they call a cab. It happens all the time. There were seven cars left on our lot last night, Mr. Stone. How was I supposed to know if one was hers? I swear to you I knew nothing. I was only out to have a good time."

"Celeste," Max said gently, "do you know where Nathan Anderson is right now?"

"No sir," she hesitated and drew a breath, "I don't. Like I said, he stayed until about ten this morning and said he had some business to take care of. I don't know what kind of business or what he meant by it."

"Do you know how to get in touch with him?"

"No sir, he didn't give me his phone number or anything."

The thought of morals crossed Max's mind. Sitting right in front of him was a woman who liked to pick up strange men, take them home, and have no-strings-attached sex with them. To make things worse, she didn't care enough to get his phone number? They probably didn't even use protection. Talk about sexual roulette.

"Ok, when the two of you left together, were you together until ten this morning?"

"Yes, he followed me to my apartment and never left there until this morning."

"Did he act nervous, distant, or funny in any way?"

"Well," she thought what an odd question to ask, "I barely know him so I don't know how he acts normally but I would say he acted normal. He was fine, didn't act nervous, well, a little nervous when we went to bed. Some guys are just nervous that way, if you know what I mean," she said playfully, her composure coming back to her now.

Max rolled his eyes, "Yes, thank you, but that's not what I meant."

"Sorry, detective. I was just trying to lighten the mood."

Max was not amused.

"John," Max looked at his partner, "do you have any further questions for Miss Schneider at this time?"

"No, Max, I can't think of anything else we need to cover right now," he answered.

"Ok, Miss Schneider, that's all we have for you for right now. I would like to reserve the right to ask you more questions, should they arise."

"Sure, no problem."

Max indicated to his partner the interview was concluded.

"The time is now," John looked at his watch as he spoke, "4:45 p.m. and this concludes the recorded interview with Miss Celeste Schneider." He turned the recorder off.

Max stood and threw a ten dollar bill on the table. "This will cover our drinks. Throw whatever is left into your tip jar."

He took a card from his wallet and shoved it toward her. "Here is my card. If you can think of anything that might be helpful to this investigation, please don't hesitate to contact me or Detective Thompson, Ok?"

"Yes, sir, but I have a question."

"Yes?"

"Am I free to go?"

"You are free to go. I would, however, stay away from Nathan Anderson. Don't make any contact with him. Also, I wouldn't plan on any trips as we may need to talk with you further."

She agreed.

Max shook her hand and thanked her for her time. John stood and followed suit.

"If we need anything more, Miss Schneider, we will be in touch," Max said.

"Thank you Detective, both of you."

"Oh," Max said as an afterthought, "you are willing to take a polygraph test, aren't you?"

Her eyes darted. "Uh, yeah, sure, whatever you need."

Suddenly, her eyes flashed with horror. "Oh my God!" she exclaimed.

Both detectives answered in unison. "What?"

"It just dawned on me. I told Nathan I was getting off work around midnight tonight. He's told me he may come and see me."

Chapter 8

Brisk air chased them to the car as they left the restaurant. The gray clouds had thickened; giving notice a decline in the weather was imminent.

Max jumped into the passenger side and slammed the door. "Shit," he said as he glanced at his watch.

What is it?" John asked, slamming his own door.

"It's a little after 5:00. We're supposed to be dining with the girls soon and we still need to go to the Lawrence's."

"Well, we've had a long fuckin' day. You wanna call it quits and put the Lawrence's off?"

"We can't do that. We've already pushed them back."

"Yeah, but, we now have a prime suspect. Hell, we even know when and where he's going to be. I say we just go have some dinner and pound a few drinks, come back here tonight and apprehend the son-of-a-bitch."

"I agree we come back here later tonight and pick him up for questioning but we need to go to the Lawrence's home.

Granted, it doesn't look good for him but when it comes down to it, it's all circumstantial. We can't hang our hat on this and quit doing our job."

"I agree."

"Besides that, they will likely know more about him since he was dating their daughter."

"I agree."

Max turned to John. "If your daughter was murdered, wouldn't you want to know someone cared?"

"Jesus H. Christ. I said I agreed with you."

"Well, I'm glad you see it my way," Max said joking. "You call Shawn and I'll call Leah. We'll tell them we're running late and we will meet them at the restaurant by 7:30."

John pulled out his cell and dialed Shawn. He started the car and pointed it toward the Lawrence's home, while Max made his call.

They arrived at the home Dan and Vivian Lawrence; a well-kept, ranch-style brick home. John pulled the car into the driveway and parked behind a tan Cadillac.

They were greeted at the door by two very distraught and tearful parents. They appeared, to Max's best guess, to be in their mid to late forties.

Max flashed his badge, "Mr. and Mrs. Lawrence, I'm Detective Max Stone, and," he motioned to John, "this is my partner Detective John Thompson. We apologize for our tardiness."

"Come in Detectives," Dan said.

They entered into the foyer and shut the door behind them. They were promptly led to the living room.

"Please have a seat," Mr. Lawrence invited.

The two sat on a large brown leather sofa across from the Lawrence's.

Vivian Lawrence had been silent until now. "Can I get you two gentlemen anything to drink or anything. It's no trouble," she added to assure them.

"No, thank you ma'am," Max said.

"We are terribly sorry about the loss of your daughter. I promise we will find the person who did this to her," Max assured them.

They nodded.

Max opened a pocket sized notepad and drew out a pen. "Again," he started, "I apologize, but this is necessary to do as soon as we can."

"We understand, Mr. Stone," Mr. Lawrence said as he slid beside his wife on the loveseat across from the detectives. He reached for her hand and gave her a reassuring squeeze.

"Your daughter did have some cash on her," Max said as he handed an envelope to Mr. Lawrence.

"Thank you, Mr. Stone," he said. His hand shook as he took the envelope.

"We were able to gather some basic information about your daughter from the I.D. carried in her purse. We know she was twenty-one and a student. Can you tell me more about her school?"

Mr. Lawrence turned to his wife for answers.

"She was a junior and was studying Biology," she said.

"Was she a full-time student?"

"Yes."

"What was her discipline?"

"What do you mean?"

"Was she specializing in a particular field in biology?"

"Oh, she was interested in genetics. She wanted to use it to help people. In fact, she just went to a seminar last weekend about organ transplants or something like that."

Max made a mental note. Something was clicking in his head but he wasn't sure what.

"Our investigation has led us to believe she was out last night with a man named Nathan Anderson."

"Yes, she was," Mr. Lawrence said.

"That's her boyfriend," Mrs. Lawrence added.

"What's your assessment of him?"

"He's a bum."

"Oh, Dan, he's a nice boy," Vivian corrected her husband.

"Have you ever seen any signs of violence from him?"

"No, I don't think Nathan would ever hurt Misty. Do you think so, Dan?"

He shrugged his shoulders.

"How long have they been dating?"

"About eight months."

"Do you happen to have a picture of him?"

She thought for a moment, "Yes!" she exclaimed, "Misty has a picture of the both of them on her nightstand."

"Can I have that picture for now?"

She excused herself and returned a moment later with a photograph containing both her daughter and Nathan Anderson.

"Thank you, Mrs. Lawrence," Max said as she handed him the photo.

She returned to her seat.

"Do you know where he lives?"

"He lives on the north-side of town in the Sol Terrace apartments, but I don't know what apartment number."

Max scribbled the information on his pad. He was familiar with the Sol Terrace apartments. A lot of illegal activity took place there and he and John had been there many times.

"Does your daughter have an address book that, perhaps, might have his address in it?"

"I don't think so, but I went shopping once with Misty and we stopped there. When you turn into the complex, you go around to the first right, or was it the second?"

"It's ok, Mrs. Lawrence. We have other ways we can find an address on him. Can you tell me anything you may recall about last night?"

"Misty left here last night around seven o'clock." She looked to her husband as if to confirm the time.

He agreed.

"She was going to meet Nathan somewhere for dinner and listen to a band." Her brow furrowed. "I'm sorry, Mr. Stone, I don't remember the name. She said the name of it, but I, just don't remember. I do remember it had a strange and unusual name."

"Was it the Rathskeller?"

"Yes! That's it."

"Since she met him there, I assume she drove herself."

"Yes."

"You're certain she met him at the restaurant?"

"Yes, I'm certain."

"Any chance she could have picked him up and drove them both to the restaurant?"

"I guess there's always a chance but I remember her telling me she was meeting him there."

"So, when she left here last night at seven, was the last time you saw or heard from her?"

"Yes," Mrs. Lawrence said. She let a tear escape.

Mr. Lawrence just pulled his wife closer to comfort her; or perhaps, it was for his own comfort.

Max and John glanced at each-other. They knew this was hard on the grieving parents, but equally knew it was important to gather information while thoughts and memories were fresh; the quicker the leads, the hotter the trail.

"Neither of you found it unusual that she didn't come home last night?"

"No, not at all, She often stays at Nathan's apartment on the weekends," Mr. Lawrence said. "She is twenty-one, Mr. Stone," he added to defend himself against judgment.

"Well, we appreciate you meeting with us today," Max said as he handed his card to Mr. Lawrence. "If you think of anything that might be important, please don't hesitate to call me. We'll be in touch."

They shook hands and left. Max and John were rudely greeted by a cold misting rain when they opened the door to go out.

"You gotta love this Indiana weather, hey buddy?" Max chuckled.

"No shit!" John answered.

They raced to John's car and made a sigh of relief upon entering.

"Damn," John said with a shiver, "that shit's cold!"

Max laughed, "It'll sure take the lead out of the pencil. Or worse, give a feller some serious shrinkage."

Max glanced at his watch. The interview went quicker than he had anticipated; that, along with his phone call to Leah about them being late, bought them some time. He pulled out his cell, looked up the number to Sol Terrace apartments, and dialed the office.

"Head to the apartment complex," Max ordered.

"We're gonna try to nail his ass now, aren't we?"

Max nodded his head as he spoke into the phone.

A few moments later, he hung up, receiving the information he was seeking.

They were just a few blocks from the Lawrence's home when John turned to Max. "Stoney, you knew the answer to damn near every question you were asking them."

"Yeah, so?"

"Why?"

"You mean, why did I ask questions I knew the answer to?"

"Yeah."

"I needed to know what they knew."

"What do you mean?"

"I wanted to make sure their story jived with what I knew, especially Dan Lawrence."

"Bullshit. You wanted to see his reaction to certain questions. You didn't have to re-hash things. You have a suspicion."

Max grinned.

"You think the dad…"

"I didn't say that," Max interrupted.

"So, what are you saying?"

"I'll let you know."

Chapter 9

John pointed the car toward the north side of town. Destination: Nathan Anderson's apartment. The drive would take about thirty minutes, maybe longer this time of day. Max took this opportunity to call Leah to tell her they had had one more stop to make and they should be at the restaurant around 7:30. He asked her if she could just meet them at Sanqunetti's for dinner as planned. Otherwise, if he and John had to go back to the station to pick up his car, it would be much later. She was used to plan changes. They seemed to come often due to Max's job. She happily agreed, even offering to have the wine waiting.

John took the opportunity to phone his girlfriend, Shawn, to ask her the same. She agreed. She would hang out with Leah, you know, girl talk, as she put it.

"Got that taken care of," Max said as he hung up his phone. "Things cool on your end Tank?"

"No Problem."

"Great!" Max collected his thoughts for a moment and said, "You got a feel on this Nathan Anderson?"

"Well, I don't want to jump to conclusions, but it's definitely not looking too good for him."

Max nodded his head. "I know what you mean." A moment later he added, "You know, though, they never go this easy." He chuckled.

"I know. We never get a break. Here it is Friday evening, we both have dinner dates with our ladies, but what are we doing?" He paused for a moment. "We're chasing down bad guys."

"Let's collect our evidence here. Let's go over what we know."
"Shoot."

"Our main suspect is Nathan Anderson?" Max started.

"Correct," Tank responded.

"Why did he kill her?"

"We know from the blood work that she wasn't pregnant so that would lead us to young Celeste Schneider," Tank said.

"Would a man kill a woman over another?" Max asked.

"Of course, it happens all the time."

"Ah, but for a woman he just met?"

"But is it a ruse? Are the two in it together? Could it have been a plot to take Misty out?"

"Good point, but if that is true, she sure cooperated a lot with us and, without an attorney."

"Unless," Tank said as if it were a fact, "Celeste helped him get rid of Misty and then she turns on Nathan. She gets rid of both that way."

"Possible, but I think we need to start at the root and not get too far-fetched."

"Yeah, I agree. Why are we reaching?"

"Here's what I think so far," Max said. "Nathan is with Misty and they go out. Next, Nathan, who is obviously a piece of work, meets Celeste, a woman who he thinks is sexier than what he has. Next, he realizes he has a chance with Celeste but needs to get rid of Misty. Well, Misty isn't going down without a fight. She sees Nathan and Celeste flirting at the bar and she gets raging mad. The two get into a fight. She's seen causing a ruckus in a public place, which had to be very embarrassing for Mr. Nathan Anderson. He gets even angrier and forcefully drags her out of the bar around 10 p.m. He is gone for about two and a half hours. During this time, nobody knows of his whereabouts, as far as we know, until he comes back to the bar at 12:30 a.m. for Celeste."

"I agree with all that, Max. But why the hell would he kill her? Why not just dump her?"

"Good question. I haven't figured that one out yet. Perhaps, he was so embarrassed by her at the bar his anger took over and he lost control. Who knows? Hopefully, he will supply the answer when we nail his ass."

For the next few moments, the two rode in silence. Max's theory was good, maybe too good. He felt strongly, though somewhere deep inside of him, that Celeste was not involved. That part of it just didn't feel right to him. She was too free with her answers. Or, she was damn good at deception. Max had many years as a detective and was considered among the best. He wasn't easily fooled. He was an expert at reading a person and Celeste Schneider seemed genuine. Max believed she was just a promiscuous woman looking to have some fun, even if it was at the expense of another woman. He believed she was concerned with nothing more than possibly breaking a heart or two.

The sun was now below the horizon now and, with the gray sky, the mist, and the low-lying clouds, it cast an eerie bloody color on the bottom side of the clouds.
Max pointed to the apartment as the two approached. "There," he said, "that one there."

John pulled the car into the apartment complex and parked. They quickly made their way to Nathan's apartment. They knocked several times, but there was no answer.

John walked around to the back of the building, while
Max stayed to watch the front. In the back, John discovered a balcony with a sliding glass door. He climbed the stairs to the second floor and peered inside. He tried to open the door, but it was locked.

The neighborhood was strangely quiet, especially for a Friday evening. John strained his ears for any sign of life from within the apartment. His concentration was so fixed on the task at hand, he didn't notice that a man had crept to, and was standing at, the foot of the stairs.

Moments passed, without incident, as the stranger watched.

Max was still on the front side of the building. He fumbled through his jacket pocket, searching for the slip of paper that Vivian Lawrence had given him, that held Nathan Anderson's phone number. Finding it, he made a few phone calls to the apartment as he stood outside the door. He could hear the phone ringing. He strained his ears to see if he could hear any movement from inside. He knocked once again. No answer. He wondered if Nathan was, in fact, inside the apartment, unwilling to answer the door or phone. Could he have been tipped off by Celeste Schneider?

John stood at the back door, his ears strained against the glass for any signs of life. He decided it was futile. To his left, a streetlight switched on, as dusk gave way to darkness. The mist had let up, but left the nighttime air thick and heavy with moisture. In the distance, the yapping of a dog was the only sound that reached his ears. He turned to descend the stairs. It was then he discovered the stranger and found himself staring down the barrel of a locked and loaded pistol.

Chapter 10

"Hold it right there, mister," the darkened figure demanded.

John froze in an instant and instinctively raised his hands. His eyes strained through the dark mist in an attempt to see the stranger. The streetlamp provided no more than a shadowy outline. "Are you Nathan Anderson?" John asked in an even and steady voice.

"I'll ask the fucking questions. Who are you and what do you want?" The tone of his voice was commanding and unwavering.

"Sir," John raised his voice a little, "I am Detective John Thompson of the I.P.D. Are you Nathan Anderson?"

"Right," the stranger said with sarcasm.

"If you'll just let me show you my badge," John said as he started to reach inside his jacket.

"Stop! I'll shoot you!"

John instantly returned his hands to a raised position.

"Why are you snooping around here?" the stranger asked.

"Sir," John said with aggravation, "I am looking for Nathan Anderson. I need to talk to him. Are you him?"

"Why? What's it about?" the faceless voice said.

Suddenly, Max put the end of Raven, his 357-Magnum, to the back of the stranger's head and cocked the trigger. "One twitch and you're in hell," he said sternly through gritted teeth. "Drop that pistol to the ground and slowly turn around," he commanded.

The stranger lowered his weapon and dropped it. He raised his hands and turned. He eyes locked with Max's cold gray eyes.

"Don't shoot me mister," he pleaded. "I don't want any trouble. Please, take what you want, just don't hurt me."

"Bullshit," Max barked. "That man just told you he was a detective."

John had since made his way down the stairs to the front of the man.

"I'm sorry, mister, but you never know if someone is telling the truth or not. I was only trying to protect my property." the frightened man stuttered.

John removed his badge from the inside of his jacket and shoved it in the man's face. "Look at it you bastard!" he commanded. "What does it say?" John spat as he pressed the silver badge to the man's face.

"And I'm Detective Max Stone."

"I'm sorry!" the man pleaded.

"What are you doing outback? Were you expecting us? Did Celeste Schneider tip you off?" Max asked in rapid succession.

"Uh, no I, uh, I don't know a Celeste Schneider."

"Bullshit!" Why else would you be out here in the dark, trying to get a jump on us Nathan?"
"I'm not Nathan. I'm his roommate, Leon Stutz."

"Well, we will just see about that." John picked up the discarded pistol, placed it in his jacket, took out his handcuffs, and cuffed the man standing in front of him. Then, he reached inside the man's back pants pocket and removed his wallet to check his I.D. "Well, Mr. Stutz," John said as he checked the information on the license, "you have a ton of explaining to do."

"Start with, where's Nathan Anderson?" Max demanded.

"I don't know. I haven't seen him since about midnight last night," Leon said. "What did he do?"

"We want to talk with him about the murder of Misty Lawrence."

"Misty's dead?" Leon exclaimed.

"I'm afraid so," Max replied. "Do you know anything about it?"

"No! No!" he said while shaking his head.

"Tell us what you do know, Leon," Max asked calmly.

"All I know is Nathan came home last night around

11:30. He went straight to the shower, got dressed, and left around midnight, like I said."

"What was his demeanor," John asked.

"He was in a really good mood. He said he had broken up with Misty but had met a really sexy woman and was going back to her apartment to get laid."

"And he hasn't been back since?"

"No, I swear," he pleaded.

"You said he took a shower. Did he change clothes?" Max asked.

"Yeah, sure he did. Why?"

"Mr. Stutz, may we have a look around the apartment?" Max said to the handcuffed man.

Leon shook his head. "I don't know," he said with hesitation, "I think I might need an attorney to advise me or something."

"Mr. Stutz," John barked, "you do realize that you pointed a loaded weapon at a police officer. Do you know what can happen to you?" He paused for a moment and drew a quick breath. "Now, Mr. Stone and I might be a little more willing to look the other way if you cooperate with us unless, of course, you are concealing information and evidence."

"If I let you go inside will you let me go?"

Max was about to respond to his request when three squad cars came racing into the complex and around to the back with lights flashing. Max quickly took out his badge and held it and his pistol above his head. John raised his badge as well.

The lead car skidded to a stop and an officer jumped out. "Freeze," he said, drawing his revolver.

Max recognized the officer as Corporal Joe Englewood. "Joe," Max shouted, "I am Detective Max Stone. My badge is in my hand in plain sight."

The officer shined a spotlight on the detective and learned he actually recognized him as well. He withdrew his revolver. "Sorry, detective, we had a call of a holdup." He approached the three men as Max and John lowered their hands and went about their business. "Do you need assistance, Detective?"

"Last chance Leon," John said softly in his ear.

"Ok, ok, I give you permission to enter the apartment," Leon reluctantly agreed.

"Actually, Joe, yes I could use your help," Max said.

Officer Englewood sent the other two squad cars on their way. "How can I help, sir?" he asked.

"I want you to watch this apartment. We are currently looking for a man by the name of Nathan Anderson. If he comes here, you arrest him and get in touch with me through dispatch."

He agreed and left to take up a position of observation.

"Ok, Leon, let's go see what we can find inside," John said as he led him up the stairs. Max followed.

"Aren't you gonna take the hand cuffs off of me?"
"Not a chance. Not until we're done." John said as he fished the keys out of Leon's pocket. He unlocked the patio door and they entered. Leon told them where they could

find Nathan's room as John positioned him on the couch. "Move a muscle and Max will have to kill you. Do you understand?"

Leon nodded.

They entered the slipshod bedroom. Five or six empty cans of Coke sat on the nightstand next to a photo of Misty. The glass on the frame had been broken. The bed was left unmade and the sheets looked like they hadn't been changed in a month. The walls were adorned with a few playboy centerfolds, the carpet desperately needed a vacuum ran over it, and the room had a slight smell of stale marijuana.

"Jesus Christ," Max said with disgust, "this man's a freakin' slob. Judging by the Lawrence's home, how the hell could someone like Misty Lawrence get mixed up with someone like this?"

John shook his head but said nothing.

It took the two detectives no time to find what they were looking for; the clothes Nathan had on the night before. Max carefully looked the crumpled clothing over. He discovered a few splatters of blood on the green shirt he was wearing and a drop or two on the jeans he had worn.

"Bingo!" John exclaimed as Max showed him the stains.

A big grin crept across Max's face. "Looks like a very bad sign for Mr. Anderson, don't you think?"

The two collected the evidence. Max took out his cell phone and called in a sweeper team, a forensic group of officers whose sole purpose is to collect evidence, even microscopic, like hair and blood samples, at crime scenes.

The team arrived a few minutes later. Max gave them the clothes and instructed them to thoroughly sweep the room and get their findings to Terry Green as quickly as possible.

"Leon," Max said, "it's your lucky day. I think Detective Thompson and I can forgive it this time." Max turned to John, "Take the cuffs off him."

Leon was visibly shaken by the sudden rush of police activity in his apartment. He rubbed his wrists as John removed the cuffs.

"Mr. Stone," he said just before the detectives reached the door, "if I see Nathan, I will call the police. I liked Misty and, to be honest with you, she was way too good for him."

They nodded in a gesture of thanks and left.

Max looked at his watch, "Shit, it's nearly 7! Let's call it a day and go meet the ladies for dinner. We're going to be late as it is."

John agreed.

Chapter 11

Max phoned Leah to let her and Shawn know they were on their way. She was disappointed to learn he and John were going to be about thirty minutes late, but knew it was unavoidable. Max had had a hellish day and really wanted nothing more than a quick dinner and to go home to bed with her. No chance of that happening. However, he had been looking forward to this night out with his wife and friends all week. And later, go back to the Rathskeller to see if Nathan Anderson showed up there.

They made a quick stop at a grocery chain, each picking up a single long-stem, red rose, and quickly made their way to the restaurant.

John sped into the parking lot of Sanqunetti's and found the first parking space he could. The frigid air and icy rain smacked Max in the face like a thousand stinging hornets, as he and John raced to the door. Puddles of water had formed in the low spots on the asphalt from the light rain that had been falling over the last hour. Max cussed as he smacked his shoe right in a puddle, splashing cold water on his trouser leg.

"Hello, gentlemen, welcome to Sanqunetti's. My name is Allison. How many will be dining in your party this evening?"

"Actually, Allison, there are four of us, but our ladies should be seated and waiting for us," Max said.

"No problem, sirs. Are you two Mr. Stone and Mr. Thompson?"

"I must be," Max quipped. "No one else wants to be me." She grabbed two menus. "Follow me, please."

The restaurant was alive and vibrating with the sounds of happy people talking, laughing, enjoying good food, and enjoying life. This was much better, Max thought. This was a stark contrast to how his day had been. He felt the tension leave his body and he could finally quit being Max Stone, Detective, and become, well, Max Stone, even if only for a little while.

"How are you gentlemen this evening?" Allison asked as she led them to the waiting women.

"Allison," Max boasted. "You wouldn't believe the day we've had even if told you."

She turned and smiled. "I'm sorry to hear you had such an unlucky day, but I bet your wives must be lucky to have someone think enough of them to bring them roses."

"Oh, I'm not married," John blurted.

Max nudged him in the side and told him to quit flirting. John smiled back and flipped him the finger and then proceeded to make lustful gestures towards Allison behind her back.

"What my idiot friend meant was, thank you Allison," Max apologized. He was fighting to hold back a chuckle. John, on the other hand, was about to lose it.

"Here we are gentlemen," she directed with her hand.

Leah and Shawn stood and greeted the two men with an embrace, which preceded a small kiss.

Leah looked dressed to kill with pink corduroys that clung to her brilliant bottom and a low-cut, white, lacy top sporting spaghetti straps. Shawn was equally stunning wearing a pale-yellow top and tight black jeans. Her jeans had a wide strip of white lace down the outside of each pant leg, teasing one's eyes with an occasional glimpse of tanned flesh.

"For you, my lady," Max said as he presented his rose like a gallant knight.

"And you, my lady," John said while presenting his gift to Shawn.

Both women, as if rehearsed, curtseyed and happily accepted their rose. Then they returned to their seats. The two men remained standing.

"Two beautiful roses for two beautiful women," John added.

"Yeah, if we only had a drink to toast," Max joked as he looked around.

As if on cue, a waitress approached with two icy cold beers. Paulaner: A delicious German wheat beer. Max's favorite.

A devilish grin crept across Max's face as she approached. He gave her a quick look-over. She was attractive with long curly brunette hair with blond highlights. Her face was painted with perfect makeup that showed-off her beauty, rather than masking flaws. Everything was in the right place, as far as Max was concerned. The nametag on her uniform read, Marcy.

"An angel is a beautiful brunette carrying Paulaner," Max said aloud to the table as she arrived.

She showed signs of embarrassment as her cheeks turned a light pink. Leah, Shawn, and John all laughed.

"Here you are sirs," Marcy said. She placed an icy-cold brew in each man's open, waiting hand. Then she placed frosted beer glasses on the table where they would be sitting. Before she left, Max ordered two more bottles and a couple of shots of Red Stag bourbon.

"Honey, the tone in your voice told me this was not a wine kind of evening for you so Shawn and I took the liberty of ordering you guys a Paulaner. I hope you don't mind," she said with a flirtatious grin.

"God, I love this woman!" He turned to his buddy. "Did I tell you I love this woman?"

"Let's drink to love," John said.

Both tipped their bottle and took a long, refreshing pull.

"Now, will you two idiots sit down?" Shawn pleaded.

"Yeah, yeah," John said. "In a moment, honey."

Max raised his beer, made a toast to friendship, and the two tipped their brown-colored bottles again.

"Ahh, Paulaner is the nectar of the Gods," Max proclaimed.

"You know, Stoney, now that you mention it, I bet God would drink Paulaner if he drank beer."

"God, Leah," Shawn said leaning across the table, "are they always like this?" she said laughing.

"I'm afraid so," Leah answered.

Shawn shook her head, "Are you two idiots going to sit down sometime tonight? You are making a scene."

"Well, shit, I guess we better sit down, Stoney," John said.

They finally took their seats.

Max poured the remainder of his beer into the frosted mug that awaited him. The orange-amber color of the malted wheat beer filled the glass. Before pouring all the contents out of the bottle, he swished the remaining beer around and poured again.

"What are you doing?" Shawn asked with curiosity. She wondered if Max had lost his mind.

"He's getting the wheat out of the bottom of the bottle," Leah answered for her husband.

She had witnessed this ritual a thousand times before. Shawn looked at her as if she were crazy. Leah understood. She used to think it was crazy as well.

"Seriously," Leah reaffirmed.

"It's true, Shawn," Max said. "You see, German wheat beers, especially unfiltered ones like this one, have wheat settlement in the bottom of the bottle. It's kind of brown in color. See?"

She watched as drops of brown fluid dripped onto the foam on top of his glass.

"Oh my God, I've never seen anything like that." She pointed at the drops coming out of the bottle.

"Of course not, because most American beers from the major breweries are not unfiltered wheat beers. They're something else like a Pilsner." Max took another drink from his glass. "This shit's good! Here, try it."

John and Leah both got grins on their face as Shawn pulled the glass to her lips and sipped.

The look on Shawn's face was priceless. "I don't know about that," she said as she tried desperately to get the look of disgust off her face. "It's different, I'll give you that."

"It takes some getting used to. It is an acquired taste. Now, I can't even taste those wimpy beers. This is a true beer, brewed the true way." He finished by savoring more of the brew.

"Say it, preacher man," John laughed with raised glass. "I have to drink to that." He drank.

"Shawn," Leah said as she patted her friend's hand, "we are in for a long night."

Shawn rolled her eyes. Max and John sipped their beers.

Marcy appeared with two fresh beers; just in time for Max as he was emptying the last drink from his glass.

He surveyed the half-empty bottle of Chardonnay on the table, "You ladies need more wine?"

"Not this round, but probably by the next round," Leah said. She reached for her near empty glass as if the question was a suggestion to drink.

"Suit yourself."

He turned to the waitress as she placed the beers, along with new frosty glasses, on the table. Next to the beers, she placed the shots of bourbon. "Marcy, we've all had really bad day. This $50 is for you, in advance," he said as he placed the money into her hand. "If you take good care of us and put up with our crap, and maybe even humor us a little, I'll put another $50 with it at the end of the evening. Fair enough?"

Marcy's eyes popped with disbelief. Before she could agree and thank him, John also shoved a $50 into her hand and agreed to add an additional $50 at the end of the evening.

"Yes sir; both you sirs," she bubbled.

"Nope, that's not going to cut it." Max joked. "We're all friends here. Let me introduce you. This is Leah." He gestured to his wife. "These folks are John and Shawn." He motioned in their direction. "But, his friends call him Tank. And my name is Max, but my friends call me Stoney."

"Ok," she said. "It's a pleasure to meet all of you. Can I get you an appetizer or anything sir, I mean Max?" she corrected herself.

"Well," Max said. He dipped his head as if he were offended and looked at John. "I guess we're not friends."

Marcy huffed playfully. "May I get the table any appetizers Stoney?"

Max was satisfied. "Ah, much better, Marcy."

He polled the table. The consensus was to order whatever he thought. He turned to Marcy. "How's the calamari?"

She wrinkled her nose. "Icky and fishy." She frowned at the thought of the fried squid.

"I like her," Max said to the table. "Wonderful, we'll have that," he said. He sought approval from the table, which he received.

"Very good," she replied, "I'll put that order in for you right now." She started to walk away, but turned back to the table and grinned, "Am I to assume to continue bringing beers or should I wait for you to order them?"

"You would be correct, Marcy. Keep bringing them until John here passes out," he joked.

He received a hearty laugh from all.

"Here's to great friends and great times," Max said as he lifted his freshly poured glass.

The other three lifted their glasses in unison and all four clinked like the sound of a bicycle bell ringing.

"So, honey," Max said while lowering his glass, "did you save the world today?"

"Getting closer," she chuckled. "I know I'm on the verge of a major breakthrough. I'm confident all I'm missing is just one piece of the puzzle and soon, surgeons around the world will be replacing damaged bodily organs with new organs that are produced from the patient's own D.N.A.," she said with pride.

"It's hard to believe science has come that far," John said.

"Yeah, it's some wild shit," Max added. "My baby girl here has been working on..." He turned to her. "What is it again, baby?"

Leah laughed and decided to bail him out. "Embryonic stem cells."

"That's a mouthful," John said while sipping his beer.

"I think it's wonderful, Leah, that you will be responsible for adding life to potentially terminal people. What a gift you are giving," Shawn said with admiration.

"Thank you, but it's not complete yet," Leah cautioned. "I should have some preliminary results from my latest experiment in a few weeks."

"Well, we will all keep our fingers crossed baby," Max said. Then he winked at her.

"Yeah, if I can just keep that asshole, Doug Brewer, out of my business," she said.

"Is that son-of-a-bitch still giving you problems at work?"

"What?" John asked. "What's this?"

"Oh, some dick weed at work; this Dr. Doug Brewer, has been giving her problems," Max said.

"How so?"

"Leah is smarter than he is, and much younger. This guy has been a scientist for like forever. He can't stand the fact that she is in charge of this research project and that she is on the verge of a major breakthrough. It's all top-secret, so Leah can't reveal anything about how she arrived at the formulas she is using. He is trying to pry it out of her. Hell, I don't even know, although it wouldn't matter if she did tell me." He smiled. "Like I would understand it anyway."

Everyone laughed.

"So, what you have is a jealous prick?" John asked.

"Exactly," Leah agreed.

"But the good side," Shawn interjected, "is that no matter who discovers it, the end result is life. Right?"

"Leah smiled at her friend, "Exactly, but Dr. Brewer doesn't quite see it that way."

"Let's drink to assholes!" John proclaimed, lifting his glass.

"You'd drink to a turd, Tank," Max joked as he raised his glass.

"You're point being?" John poked back.

The women followed suit and once again they drank together.

Marcy appeared with a plate of fried calamari and placed it in the middle of the table. She also placed two more bottles of beer, with frosty mugs, on the table; one in front of Max and the other in front of John.

"Thank you, Marcy," Max said. "Next trip, better bring another bottle of Chardonnay for the ladies," he said as he reached over and filled the ladies wine glasses, draining the bottle.

"I'll take care of that, Stoney. Are you ready to order?" she asked as she pulled out her order pad.

Everyone was, so Marcy started with the ladies and worked her way around the table, writing as she went: Double-cut rack of lamb, served medium rare for Max, crab cakes for Leah, lobster ravioli with shrimp for Shawn, and pasta Sanqunetti for John. She thanked them, collected their menus, then left to place their orders and to get a fresh bottle of wine.

"So, honey, tell us about your guy's day. You ran out of the house so quickly this morning. I haven't really gotten to talk to you all day," Leah said as she sipped her wine.

"Oh," John interrupted. "I meant to tell you, Leah. I'm sorry about the interruption in your plans this morning." He let a devilish grin sweep across his face.

Max was trying to conceal his laughter.

"Kiss it, Tank," she said with her own fiendish demeanor as she leaned and pointed to her butt. "I'll get even with you."

"Oh, I'm so scared," he said while wiggling his fingers. "Honey, you don't really want to hear about our day. It was long and we're not even done," Max answered.

"What do you mean, you're not done?"

"We have a pretty good suspect from a murder we investigated this morning and we think we know where he will be around midnight or so, and we need to go check it out."

Shawn and Leah wanted to know more. Max and John were reluctant but gave some minor details. Even those were disturbing to the women. The four sipped drinks and continued to talk about their day. Marcy showed with a fresh bottle of wine for the ladies and another round of beer for the men.

"Right on time," Max joked with her.

She addressed the table as she placed the beverages in front of each. "Your dinner will be out soon."

"Thank you, no rush," Max said.

She flashed a brilliant smile and dismissed herself.

The four friends resumed their conversation, enjoying their time together. Soon, the calamari was devoured and the conversation turned upbeat once again, as the effects of the alcohol started setting in. The usual joke jousting began, as each tried to out-do the other with the latest and greatest joke they had heard. Some were clean, but most were dirty. Even Shawn, who was always cooped up in an office, as a legal secretary, got in a few good ones. Yes, even attorneys have a sense of humor.

Before they knew it, twenty minutes had passed and Marcy was returning with a fresh round of drinks and their dinner.

Max inhaled deeply over his plate and allowed the wonderful aroma of his herb crusted rack of lamb embrace his nostrils. It smelled heavenly. He slid the blade of his knife between two of the bones and carved into the juicy, tender lamb, exposing the pinkish-red flesh of the medium-rare meat. He was anticipating his first bite like a baby awaiting his bottle. Finally, as if it was a reward, Max took a bite of the flavorful meat, savoring the delicacy.

He glanced up and noticed John and Shawn were both watching him with amusement.

Through closed lips, he smiled as he chewed for a moment, and then swallowed. "What?"

"Is it that good, Stoney?" John chuckled.

"Hell yes. You should've ordered this yourself." Max cut another chop off the rack and placed it on John's plate. "Here, try this."

"I thought for a minute there you were going to make love to it instead of eat it."

"I didn't want to make Leah jealous," he said joking.

John looked at his friend with amusement as he sampled the lamb. Max's face had to look of a child seeking the approval of his mother.

"Well, what do you think of it?"

"Hey!" John drew out slowly. "This is damn good!" He turned to Shawn. "Here honey, try this," he said while placing a forkful of it in her mouth.

She, too, agreed it was very good.

Leah watched as she ate her crab cakes. She appeared to be in heaven.

John finally turned his attention to his own dish, as did Shawn.

Conversation slowed while they enjoyed their dinner but they still managed to discuss various topics such as the latest Colt's game and how they should make the playoffs and do well. They discussed Christmas, which was quickly approaching in just about a month, and of next summer's vacation.

They were about half way through their meal when Max's cell phone rang. He checked the caller I.D. and the number was restricted. He briefly thought of ignoring the call but decided against it. It could be someone from police headquarters or from the forensic science lab with an update on his case.

"Hello, Max Stone," he answered.

He was greeted with the same sandpapered voice of the stranger, who had threatened to kill his wife a few days ago. "Guess who, Mr. Stone," the mysterious voice said. "You didn't think I forgot about you," he paused, "did you, Mr. Stone?"

Chapter 12

"Who is it, honey?" Leah asked.

Max ignored her request. She asked again with a little more persistence as she tugged on his shirt.

Max lowered the phone, "It's the forensic lab," he lied. He stood up and excused himself.

"Tell her the truth, Mr. Stone," the stranger requested. He laughed with a demonic tone that sounded like the devil laughing through a snare drum.

There was no way in hell Max was telling Leah. He would much rather have his testicles pounded flat with a wooden hammer. At first, he did consider telling her and then sending her away to her mother's for safe keeping. But, and Max was ashamed to admit it, he needed her here so this psycho cowboy would eventually show himself. Without her here, the stranger would never show. It was demoralizing and frustrating for Max. He didn't know who this person was or any identity to go by. He had no idea what the person even wanted or what he was trying to prove. He was left only with his senses and his wits to keep her alive. This whole twisted ordeal tore at his soul.

Max made his way to the bar, far away from his table, but he could still see it. He wanted to make sure he was out of ear shot.

"What is it you want this time, dickhead?" Max said into the phone.

The sandpapered voice chuckled again. "Now, now, Mr. Stone." He paused and drew a breath. "Aren't we having fun?"

"One of us is," Max barked. "Listen, asshole, why don't you show your face and you and I will make this man to man. You can leave my wife out of your sick psychotic game."

"Now, Mr. Stone," the stranger's voice was slow and deliberate, "isn't it amazing how you choose to lower yourself from your sophistication to red-neck mentality with all your verbal abuse of the English language." He was silent for a moment, then continued. "It appears, Mr. Stone, that you enjoy games as well."

Max looked in the direction of the table and noticed John was looking back at him. He knew something was up. He suspected it was the stranger, but was sworn to secrecy. He was given strict orders to tell no one; not even Shawn. Leah was used to interruptions brought on by Max's police work. She had returned, along with Shawn, to eating her dinner.

"You are the one playing games, asshole. Who are you? Are you someone I sent up? Whatever it is, it has nothing to do with my wife. So, why don't you and I have it out man to man and I'll put a bullet through that sick, twisted, mind of yours and put you out of your misery!"

The voice showed some excitement. "Now, that's the way I like you, Mr. Stone." He approved. "I want you pissed. I want you ready for a fight; a showdown if you will. I want to drive you insane, Mr. Stone." He paused. "I will succeed. And, when the time is right, you will see me."

"Why not right now? You pick the place and I will be there."

"Oh," the deep mysterious voice drew out, "I could have, Mr. Stone," he boasted. "Let me ask you a question, Mr. Stone."

"What?" Max demanded.

"Do you think it's appropriate to leave your wife and her friend sitting all alone in a restaurant for over thirty minutes?"

Max made no comment. His throat went dry. He found he couldn't swallow and, for a brief moment, he couldn't breathe.

"Mr. Stone?" the voice continued, "don't you think your wife looks hot this evening in her pink corduroys?"

Alarms sounded in Max's head. The son-of-a-bitch was in the restaurant! He took a quick look around the bar area, looking for anyone who might be on a cell phone. He saw just one, but he was with a woman. It couldn't be him.

Besides, that man was talking, but Max wasn't hearing anything on his end.

Max walked to the front of the restaurant. Still, he saw nothing. Sweat beaded on his forehead. His heart was pounding so hard, he felt it was going to rip right through his rib cage.

"Show yourself, you son-of-a-bitch," he demanded.

The mysterious voice mocked him on the other end. "Mr. Stone, I assure you, now is not the time. Oh, yes, I could have killed her tonight." He paused for a moment. "I could have killed her friend too, for that matter. But, where would the fun be in that, Mr. Stone? No, no, now is not the time. It will come, when I decide for it to. And, it will happen right under your nose."

Max's breathing had become shallow and his blood was racing through his veins so quickly, his flesh was red and warm. His temples pounded like a drum and he could hear his life-blood swishing through his ears.

"I will never let you get close to Leah," Max snapped through gritted teeth. "I will find you and I will kill you! And, when I do, the long, cold barrel of my revolver will be the last earthly thing you see before I send you to hell."

Laughter of delight echoed in the phone receiver. "Won't let me get close to her, Mr. Stone? I was within fifty feet of her. No, Mr. Stone," he retorted. "You cannot stop me. I could have done it tonight." I will strike like a ghost, Mr. Stone. I could be right beside you and you would never know. Rest assured, Mr. Stone, the time is coming and it is coming soon, but it's not coming now."

"Yes," Max agreed. "It is coming soon, for you. Make no mistake about it I will take you down," Max reiterated through clinched teeth, so tight he thought they might shatter.

"Mr. Stone, do not bother looking for me at the restaurant. You don't really think I would be stupid enough to stay now do you? I left a good ten minutes before I called you," the stranger mocked.

"I knew you were too much of a chicken-shit to play fair. You get your rocks off on this don't you?"

The strange, sandpapered voice laughed unmercifully once again. "Very clever," he paused. "Mr. Stone, I shall leave you for now, but I will be in touch. I am truly sorry for breaking up your little party," he said with wryness in his voice. "I wonder if Leah will cry and beg for her life like Misty Lawrence did."

"You killed Misty Lawrence?"

"As a matter of fact I did. Others will be killed too, but your wife will be my most precious trophy."

Max's lake-blue eyes turned cold gray with anger. "You sick bastard, you just fucked up. You think I don't know who you are, but now I do. I will get you. I'm going to rip your still-beating heart out and show it to you while you die!" Max said, nearly shouting.

"Mr. Stone?" the evil voice returned, "I accept your challenge." He paused for a few moments. "Do you know what gets my rocks off, Mr. Stone?"

Max didn't answer.

"No? Allow me to share. When a woman is tied down and helpless, and you look deep into her eyes and you see the fear. And, you know she is so afraid, right down to her soul. You caress her warm, burning cheek and tears well up in her eyes as she begs you for her life. Oh, the feeling she must have, knowing she is about to die," he said with excitement. "She promises to do anything in exchange for her life. But, what she doesn't realize is, I am in control and can do anything I want and I don't need her permission. She is shaking so bad, her brain tries to make her faint so she can escape the terror. But, she fights desperately to stay awake for fear it could be her last waking moments. She promises to be my sex slave if only I let her go. She tries to swallow, but can't when she sees the knife being pulled from my coat. I love to watch her eyes follow the blade as I slowly move it to her abdomen. She is so scared she can't even talk or move as I sink the blade into her soft flesh and slowly pull it down the side of her stomach. You know she wants to look away, but she can't. She can't believe this is happening as she watches her skin pull apart, exposing her insides, and her blood trickles across my hands. Oh, to hear her pray to her God to smite me down with a lightning bolt or something as she feels her own warm blood oozing from her body. Then, I like to watch her drift off into eternal slumber. That, Mr. Stone, is what gets my rocks off. I so hope Leah won't let me down," he laughed.

"How could you do something like that to a flesh and blood woman?"

"You see, Mr. Stone, when you reach into my chest to pull out my heart to show me, you will find that I don't have one."

Chapter 13

Max went to the bar and ordered a shot of Red Stag and gulped it down. He had many questions but no answers. Why was this man targeting Leah? Why would he call Max and torment him this way? What kind of motives did he have? Most pressing of all, if this man did kill Misty Lawrence, was it Nathan Anderson? And, if so, was he serious when he said others would die too? And, if others were going to die, was the death of Misty Lawrence over jealousy?

Hell, if it was Nathan Anderson, he was pretty ballsy. Max already had mounting evidence that fingered him, although Nathan didn't know that. Motive too. He was the last known person to be seen with Misty. He was caught by flirting with bartender by her. He was seen pulling her out of the bar, by her arm, in a fit of rage. Max would get him. He knew where Nathan was going to be later tonight, but Nathan didn't know that.

Another full bottle of Paulaner awaited Max when he returned to his table. He was still visibly shaken and his face showed the signs of worry. Leah had seen this look on his face before, but rarely. Max was tough to the core and usually hard as nails, but he had a soft, sentimental side to him that he rarely showed outside of home. She knew both sides of him and could tell when something wasn't quite right.

"Honey?" she asked with concern, "Is everything all right?" She smiled reassuringly as she placed her soft hand on top of his.

"Yeah, everything is o.k." he lied.

"You sure?" she asked again.

He smiled at his wife. "Yes, baby, I'm sure. It's just work. Gruesome details about the murder Tank and I investigated this morning, that's all."

John studied his best friend. He too, knew Max. They had been best friends since first grade back in the old neighborhood. Hell, that was over thirty years ago. Tank knew that Leah may have the benefit of being intimate with Max, but Max shared so much more with him than he ever did with her, or anybody else for that matter. Sure, she knew his intimate side better, of course, but Tank knew more than she thought. If she only knew some of the things about her precious man that he knew, it would put her panties in a wad. He knew Max was lying to her. He wouldn't ask now. No, he mustn't bring anything up. Max would tell him if he needed to know and when they were alone. So, he went along with his friend's lie.

"Was it Caption Lee?" John questioned.

Max looked up from his plate and caught the wink in Tank's eye.

"Uh, no, it was Terry Green from forensics. He made some conclusions about the murder of Misty Lawrence and wants to see us Monday morning, first thing," Max said.

"What sort of things, honey?" Leah asked.

Shawn had a look of question on her face as well.

Max held his hands up in refusal. "I don't want to share any details now. It would really mess up our good time here and kill our buzz," he said, trying to lighten the mood. "It would be a crime for us to spend all this money on booze and not get a buzz out of it."

"By God, I'll drink to that," John said in a smart-ass tone as he raised his glass.

The other 3 raised their glasses and toasted to a good buzz. Several other toasts were observed throughout the remainder of the evening, including to good friends, as the night went on as planned.

Chapter 14

After dinner, the two detectives went to their homes, grabbed quick showers, and met back at Max's house. The showers, along with two solid hours of gulping coffee, had rid their heads of the effects the alcohol. Max had caught his second wind.

The drive to the Rathskeller was a short one. They wanted nothing more than to start their weekend. Their day had been a long and draining one, but they had to jump at the chance to catch their suspect. They had a good lead in Nathan Anderson. And, if Celeste Schneider was telling the truth, they would find him there tonight. Max was hopeful they would bring quick justice to an innocent victim, and, hopefully, bring some sort of comfort to grieving parents.

They shook the icy water from their long coats as they entered the establishment and walked through another door that led into the main area. The music was thumping from the wall in another room on the right. On the left, a young lady ran a vacuum cleaner around tables that were being bussed and cleaned. A short, chubby hostess greeted them from her assigned station. It was clear she wanted to be anywhere but where she was.

"Evening, gentlemen," she said emotionless. "Welcome to the Rathskeller. Sorry, the restaurant is closed, unless you're here for the bar side with the music and stuff."

Max smirked and nodded his head at her. He looked at his partner and rolled his eyes. John grinned.

"Ok, then, you gentlemen can just go through that door there." She pointed.

Max thanked her and proceeded to the door. Once inside, they quickly made their way toward the bar to find Celeste Schneider and, with any luck, Nathan Anderson.

The club was crowded and festive. Colored laser lights flashed all around the room and a mirror ball sparkled above the dance floor sending streaks of colored lights bouncing around the darkened room. Max coughed from the smoky-thick air. He detested smoking, except for an occasional Cuban cigar with a snifter of fine brandy or a high-ball glass of bourbon.

The dance floor was packed primarily with young women, most scantily dressed, shaking their asses and chests to the cover of the song Brickhouse. The bar band was actually doing a fine job with the song, although they were a bit loud for Max's taste.

"There is so much ass in this place that even you could get laid here, Tank," Max said joking.

"True," he agreed, "but some of us can't be like you and get more ass than a toilet seat," he joked back.

The two men worked their way through the thick crowd, but not without saying "excuse me" at least a dozen times. John swore he was groped at least once.

A spiky-haired, waifish looking man stood behind the bar. "Hello gentlemen," he said in a feminine, girly voice as he pushed up his black-rimmed glasses. "Name your poison!"

If Max didn't know any better, he would have sworn the so-called man was trying to turn him on.

"Yes, we're looking for Celeste Schneider, uh, I didn't catch your name."

"Jimmy," he said in his feminine voice.

Jimmy had known Celeste for some time. The word on her was she was promiscuous, using the bar as a front for her sexual exploits. She often went home with men she had just met, but he never knew her to go home with two at a time.

"I'm afraid Celeste isn't here right now, sir," Jimmy said.

"When will she be back?" John asked.

"Gentlemen, I'm sorry," Jimmy said, "I'm not comfortable giving out any information without Celeste's permission. It just wouldn't be right," he finished with feminine body language.

"Look, Jimmy," Max said, agitated.

He was interrupted by the bartender. "Sir? You're not going to beat me up, are you?" he asked, showing fear.

"No! Hell no," Max shook his head. "Look, we are detectives with the IPD and Celeste told me this afternoon that she would be here tonight. Where is she?"

Jimmy had heard it all when it came to Celeste and her seductive activity. Hell, one night she went home with a man claiming to be an alien sent here to procreate with female humans for the advancement of the universe. "Right," Jimmy said as he winked at the detectives.

They flashed their badges for Jimmy to see. They tried to be discreet, but failed. A man sitting on a stool to their left gave a glance in their direction, picked up his beer, and walked away. He glanced over his shoulder as he did so.

"Is she in trouble," Jimmy questioned as he placed his hands on the top of the bar and leaned toward them.

"Sorry," Max said passively, "that's confidential unless, of course, you have some credentials you can flash me that would allow me to tell you about it."

Jimmy took exception to being mocked. He huffed in his girly fashion. "Sir, I will get the manager for you."

He turned and stomped off like a scorned child, and disappeared in the thick crowd. John looked around and noticed they were starting to gather some stares from patrons.

"Looks like the word's getting out the law is here," John said.

He agreed.

A few moments later, Jimmy returned with a chubby man in tow. He was an aging man, bald on top with a gray horseshoe of hair. He wore a white dress shirt with a blue stripped tie. He looked over the top of his half-rimmed glasses at Max. "Hello, I'm Sonny Brown. How can I help you?" he said as he stuck out a hand.

Max showed him his badge and extended his hand to shake. "Hello, Mr. Brown. I'm Max Stone. Is there somewhere you, my partner, and I can meet?"

He motioned with his hand for them to follow. Max and John followed him, through the sea of people, to his office. He opened the door and held it for them as they filed into the small, well-appointed office. Sonny shut the door behind them and took up a position behind his small, wooden desk. His rickety chair creaked as it bore his weight when he sat. The desk looked even smaller with Sonny's large frame sitting behind it.

"Now," he said "as I understand it, you are looking for Celeste Schneider?"

"Yes, Mr. Brown," Max said. "We are investigating the murder of one of your patrons. We believe she was abducted in your parking lot last night."

Sonny Brown's face turned to stone. "And you think Celeste had something to do with it?"

"No, we don't believe she did it. However, at this time, we cannot exclude her from having involvement. But, we believe a man she met last night may have committed this crime."

"We also believe he was to come back in here tonight to meet with her," John added.

Sonny shook his head again in disbelief. "I'm afraid, gentlemen, Celeste went home sick around 9:30 this evening."

"Did she leave with anyone?" Max asked.

"Yes." He let out a deep breath. "She told me her friend Nathan was going to pick her up."

Chapter 15

Max obtained Celeste Schneider's address and he and John headed for her apartment.

"Well, so much for her staying away from him," John said. "Yep, it looks like Miss Celeste may have tried to play us.

Obviously, she knows something she didn't tell us."

Max stepped to the door, raided his fist to knock, but hesitated at the last moment. He strained an ear to listen and heard the faint sound of voices talking on the inside.

Max motioned with his finger, "There's definitely a man in there with her. Let's cross our fingers," he whispered.

A thump came from inside the apartment, followed by laughter. A moment later, a shriek of happiness escaped Celeste's voice box.

"Damn she's feisty," John whispered.

Max held his extended forefinger to his lips to shush his partner.

A grin crept across their faces as they heard the heightened frenzy of sexual activity from the other side of the door. They heard the words *"give it to me Nathan"* come out of Celeste's mouth.

"Bingo!" John whispered, "at least we know she's with our suspect and not another hook-up."

"Well, let's get him. I want to go home soon." Max rapped loudly on the door.

The apartment got quiet in an instant and distinct sounds of scrambling were heard. A few *'oh shits'* were heard as well as a few thumps rifled through the wooden door.

Max banged on the door once again.

Sounds came from the television as it was turned on. They heard wooden planks squeak as soft footsteps approached from the other side.

"Who is it?" sounded softly from a woman's voice.

"Open up, Miss Schneider," Max said in his deep stern voice. "It's Detective Max Stone of the I.P.D."

"Uh, just a minute, detective," she said.

A few moments passed. They heard the sliding of a chain lock, then the door finally, and slowly, opened with a squeak.

The faint smell of marijuana drifted from inside. Her face showed slight surprise at their presence.

She looked completely different than when Max and John had spoken to her earlier in the afternoon. Her brunette hair was mussed, her makeup paled, and her bright red lipstick had been worn away. Her low-cut blouse and hip-hugging pants had been replaced by baggy, gray sweatpants and a white t-shirt. Max noticed she was braless. He could see the pale brown of her areolae straining against the thin, white cotton fabric. Even braless, her breast were perky and in place.

She rubbed her hazel eyes, as if sleepy. "Yes, detectives," she said. "I'm sorry I wasn't at work this evening. I had to come home because I wasn't feeling very good," she apologized.

"Where's Nathan Anderson?" Max's voice was stern.

"I have no idea, Detective Stone," she lied. "I came home around 10:30 and crashed on the couch. He hadn't come into the bar yet." Her eyes darted around to avoid contact. "I've been here since and I haven't heard from him."

"Do you mind if we come in to ask you a few more questions, Miss Schneider," Max said as he started to push his way through the door.

"Detective Stone," she said with resistance. She stepped into the doorway to block his advance. She clung tightly to the door. "Can't this wait until tomorrow. It's very late, I don't feel well, and I am tired."

"Ok, Celeste, let's cut out the bullshit. Max was forceful. "As a matter of fact, it can't wait until tomorrow."

Her face showed amazement of his rudeness. "I beg your pardon, detective?"

Max closed the distance between them. He deliberately invaded her personal space. She moved back a step, but held her grip on the door. Her eyes locked with his and neither spoke a word. It had become a chess match and she knew that Detective Stone knew more than he had said. How could she win?

"Don't you need a search warrant, Detective Stone," she finally said. A wry grin crept across her face. She had him. "Ahhh," Max said with amusement. He turned to his partner. "You hear that Tank? Young Miss Schneider here says we need a warrant." He turned back and grinned at Celeste. "Would you like to tell her why I don't need a warrant to enter her apartment?"

His response was ice cold. "Probable cause."

"Wait a minute," she stammered. "I told you today I had nothing to do with that woman getting killed or anything. Don't you believe me?"

"Miss Schneider," Max said as he leaned in, "that, uh, stench reeking from your apartment," he gestured in the air, "isn't perfume, now is it? I believe it to be marijuana."

She shuffled back and forth on her feet.

"Detective Thompson, does the suspicion of marijuana give us probably cause to enter?

"I believe it does, Detective Stone."

"I might also add," he paused for dramatic effect, "and here's the big kick in the ass for you." He smiled as he leaned in even closer. "You sure didn't sound sick when you and Nathan were giving the floor, and probably your neighbor below you, a thrill."

"It certainly was entertaining to us," Tank smiled at her with amusement.

Her heart sink. She knew she was caught.

"Now, Miss Schneider," Max continued. "The way I see it, you have two choices. You either let us in and allow us to question Nathan Anderson, or I call headquarters and bring down the drug sniffing canine unit and arrest you for drugs. Then, when we get in your apartment, we find Nathan and arrest him for suspicion of murder and we arrest you for aiding a suspected felon, obstruction of justice, and possible accessory to murder. How do you want it to go down?"

Her eyes lowered until her gaze hit the floor. Her face was flush and it she struggled with the decision of surrender. She knew if she still insisted on the warrant, there was no way in hell Nathan could sneak out. She lived on the second floor, there was only one door, and it was being blocked by two large detectives. She decided to cave. She stepped back from the entryway and gestured with her hand, inviting the two detectives in.

Max's pistol jumped into his hand as he entered. "Where is he and is he armed?"

She pointed down the hallway. "He's in my bedroom, the last door on the left, and he's not armed."

"I'll go, Stoney." John pulled his pistol and made his way down the short hallway.

John quickly found the door. He held his pistol in his right hand and slowly turned the knob with his left. He flung the door open.

"Freeze! Police!" he shouted as his revolver led him through the open doorway.

Nathan Anderson was sitting quietly on the bed. He didn't budge with the opening of the door or the command of the detective.

John ordered him to his feet and to turn and face the wall. Nathan did as instructed. He placed his hands behind his back, as if waiting for the handcuffs.

"I didn't do anything!" he finally said.

"Oh, no," John smirked, "not a thing, you lying bastard! You have the right to remain silent. I suggest you exercise that right."

This pissed Nathan off. "You tell me, detective," he shouted as the cuffs snapped around his wrist with a click. "What the hell did I supposedly do?"

"So, you have the right to remain silent but you lack the capacity. Is that it? Once you're secure, we'll talk."

Nathan did as instructed and stood in silence.

Max had the cuffs on Celeste Schneider and had her sitting on the sofa.

"Why am I being cuffed?" she protested.

"Oh, come on, Celeste," Max said in disbelief. "Do you really think I'm stupid?" He paused for a minute. "You told me point blank to my face this afternoon that you would have nothing more to do with Nathan Anderson after learning the suspicions he was under." And yet, damn if we didn't find him here with you," he paused and looked straight into her teary, hazel eyes. "We found you both together doing the horizontal floor dance."

"I swear to you, Detective Stone, I'm telling the truth. I know nothing about it," she cried. "I brought him here because he came into the bar early, said he needed to talk to me really bad."

Max sat beside her on the blue and beige checkered sofa. "Go on."

"Anyway," she continued, "he told me his roommate called his cell phone and told him the police were looking for him. He seemed really shaken so I figured the best thing I could do was to bring him here and wait for you."

"Well, certainly you told him about Misty Lawrence?" Max asked.

"Uh, yeah, but he swears he didn't do it."

"I see. And keeping him here for us, involved sexual activity?" Max asked her in disbelief.

"Uh, no, I guess not," her head sank. "It just happened."

John entered the room closely behind a handcuffed Nathan Anderson. "Very impressive Ms. Schneider," he said sarcastically. "Do you always use your sexual prowess and teary eyes to try to get your way with men?"

Max rose from the couch so John could place his suspect beside her. He did.

Her face was scarlet red with anger. She would've clawed their eyes out if she could.

"Tell me, Mr. Anderson," Max smirked, "I understand you knew we were looking for you. Do you know why?"

He sat defiantly. He wouldn't answer the question. He knew.

"Very well," Max said calmly. "Why didn't you turn yourself in? Why are you here with another woman in her apartment?"

"It's called having sex, you asshole." He glanced at the two detectives. "With a woman!" he added. "Not with a man like I'm sure the two of like to have together."

They found this amusing.

"Ah, what about Misty Lawrence?"

"Screw that bitch!" he screamed. "I don't care if I ever see that bitch again!"

Max drew close to the sofa, bent over and placed an arm on either side of the defiant man.

"Really, Mr. Anderson? Are you really going to play it that way? You already know she's dead."

"You bastards think I killed Misty?" he said, breaking his defying silence. "You son-of-a-bitches! I did not kill Misty!" He tried to get off the couch.

Max shoved him back into the cushions.

"You sit your ass right there!" Max commanded. "You get up again and I guarantee you won't like what happens."

Nathan spat in the direction of the detectives. A thousand thoughts were racing through his mind, all at the same time. He was so angry and his skin so hot he felt it would burst into flames. His heart was beating so hard his temples throbbed.

"I'm innocent of anything like that. You got no proof I killed her!" he said with more control.

"We'll get the evidence. Make no mistake about it."

Nathan spat in the direction of Max Stone once again. This time his liquid bullet hit its mark on Max's right cheek.

In a flash, Max grabbed him around the collar of his orange shirt and yanked him off the couch. The strength of Max's powerful arms lifted Nathan off the floor and face to face with the detective.

"You little son-of-a-bitch," Max said through gritted teeth.

Fear shot through Nathan Anderson. He crossed the line and he flinched in anticipation of inflicted pain.

"Max!" John reached out and grabbed him by the arm.

Max turned and looked at John and John shook his head.

Without looking, Max released the man back onto the couch. He walked into the kitchenette to clean his face and to get a drink of water.

"I just saved your ass," John said to the shaken suspect. "You get one. I won't save it again."

He understood.

"Now," John continued, "as I was about to say. We have already been to your apartment and have collected valuable evidence, including your clothes. And guess what," he said with a smirk, "they have blood on them."

His eyes went wide. "But, I didn't do anything, detective."

Max returned from the kitchen. He pointed at the suspect. "You were spotted in the Rathskeller, flirting with Celeste here. Next, you and the victim were seen in a heated argument by her." He moved his finger to Celeste.

"Yes, detective, all of that is true but I didn't kill her," he said calmly. "Sure, she was embarrassing me so I did drag her outside. She yanked away from me and I accidentally scratched her when she did. This pissed her off even more and she scratched me back on purpose. That is where the blood came from." He nodded his head as if trying to make an important point. "After that, she told me to go to hell. I told her the same and that was the last I saw her. I went home and cleaned up and went back to the Rathskeller."

"That's a very amusing story but it doesn't look good for you," he turned to Celeste, who had been very quiet during all of this, "nor you," he finished.

Her body language stiffened with this news.

"Me?" she said with disbelief. "Why?"

"For possible accessory to murder, and aiding and abetting.

Chapter 16

Max's weekend was a shitty one. Saturday morning's newspaper broke the story of the murder, complete with a big headline right on the front page. Funny how the more controversial a topic is, the more press it receives.

The paper had tabbed this as "a possible murder from an anti-abortionist" due to the graphic nature of the way young Misty Lawrence had been murdered. Additional coverage had been given to the "violence against stem cell research," because of the note that had been left at the murder scene. Max had no idea how the hell the press knew about the note.

There was no doubt, stem cell research was controversial. The University Hospital had directed a reporter to Leah for her take on stem cell research and to refute any negativity on the subject. So, she spent a few hours talking with the press. The weekend was filled with

119

murder talk, stem cell talk, and was a complete media circus. It was not the makings for a fantastic weekend.

Monday morning came much too soon for Max. He didn't get much time with his family. He cherished his weekends and did his best to keep them wide open for family time because during the week they were a family on the go. There was always scout meetings, committee meetings, basketball practices, and the list went on and on. They used their weekends to catch up with one another.

He could have taken a personal day, which he would've loved to have done, but Leah couldn't stay in bed with him anyway. Most of the time her job was just as demanding as his was.

At least this week was starting better than last week ended. They had a suspect behind bars for the murder of Misty Lawrence. All he had to do now was gather the appropriate evidence, interview possible witnesses, and tie up some loose ends.

Max entered the lobby of headquarters and was greeted with a smile, as usual, from Helen.

"Good morning, Detective Stone," rang out from her angelic voice.

"Good morning, Helen." He was all business and in a hurry. "Is John in yet?" he asked as he swept past her desk.

"Uh, no sir," she said standing as she watched him quickly pass her desk. She looked over the rim of her glasses, and raised her voice to the back of his head. "I don't believe he is."

Max stopped at the coffee pot, retrieved his *"World's best husband"* mug, and poured himself a steamy cup of brew. He noticed a copy of the morning paper sitting on the edge of a colleague's desk and snatched it up. Right on the top of the front page was a headline, *"Man and Woman Arrested for Murder of Local College Student,"* and right below it was the story Max was looking for, *"Is Stem Cell Research a Necessity?"* It included a picture of his wife. He frowned at that.

He went to his office to read the article, and was pleased with the way it was presented. He was all for the advancement of modern medicine through stem cell research, but was very much against having his wife's picture being pasted all over the paper. She enjoyed the attention, but Max felt it was an invitation to trouble, especially with organizations that were opposed to what she was doing. Against his wishes, she allowed a photo for the article, which caused a rather heated discussion between the two.

He wondered how the press always seemed to know what was going on, despite the fact important details were left out of press releases. One murder where a woman had her ovaries cut out did not make for conclusive evidence that it was about stem cell research. Perhaps there was something to it, but that had not been proven. But, if that were true, could it be Nathan Anderson? Max was working on the theory that he had murdered Misty Lawrence out of anger. Max had just finished the article when John poked his head in.

"Hey, buddy," he said cheerfully. "I see you're reading the article."

Max looked up over his paper and nodded. John entered his office and sat in a chair across from his desk. The leather creaked beneath Johns frame as he sat.

"Do you think there's any validity to the paper about a hate crime against stem cell research?" John asked.

"Maybe. Hell, who knows."

"You know what?" John was interrupted by a knock on the door.

It was Captain Lee.

"Max, have you seen?" he stopped as he noticed the paper in his hand, "Oh, I see you have seen this morning's paper." He smiled. "Good article. Your wife was very convincing."

"Thanks, Captain," he smiled. "John and I were just talking about the murder."

"Yes, great job on nabbing a suspect so quickly," the Captain acknowledged. He cocked his head. "Why are you two in here this morning? I heard you had a late night on Friday and you know you have comp time coming."

"It's ok, Captain. We'll take some time later," John said.

"Suit yourself boys. Build up the time if you like." He started to leave, stopped, and turned back to them. "Oh, I saw Terry Green from forensics this morning. He told me to tell you that the blood on Nathan Anderson's clothes was, in fact, Misty Lawrence's."

Chapter 17

Leah Stone was the celebrity of the day at work. Her friend Freda thought it was, in her words, totally awesome that her friend's picture was in the paper. She joked with Leah, asking her to autograph the paper for her scrapbook. Doug Brewer, on the other hand, was appetent.

He snatched the paper from Freda's hands, tearing it as he did so.

"Ladies," he monotone voice reverberated. "Can't we place all this nonsense behind us and get to work like we are paid to do?" He huffed as he gawked at Leah over the top of his glasses. "I mean, honestly. Does anybody really care what Miss Stone thinks about," he paused as if he were formulating his thoughts, "well, anything," he finished with a smirk.

The two women stared at him with contempt, but said nothing.

A corrupt smile swept across his face. "Hmmm, just as I expected. As it turns out, the answer is no."

This brought an immediate and angry response from Leah. She had bitten her tongue for too long, in the name of professionalism and keeping the peace. It was time she finally let him have it. "Let me tell you something," she shouted as she pointed in his direction. "Every day that Freda and I work in this laboratory, we have to put up with your mouth and your lousy attitude! Why don't you give us a break once in a while and put your rotten ego on hold."

He scoffed at her gull. He took his glasses from his face and put the end of the earpiece in his mouth, as if he was amused at her antics.

"Well, we are sick of it!" She gestured toward Freda. She moved within a step of Doctor Brewer's face. "You can go screw yourself."

His brow rose. She had some nerve. How dare she speak to him that way? Hot blood rushed to his face. If she wasn't a woman he would deck her.

"You will just have to get over the fact that I am smarter than you and younger than you!" she shouted. "And, keep in mind, I am your boss."

Freda was doing a good job holding back her excited approval. Inwardly, she applauded her friend's truthful barrage.

Leah vented more words, her voice and confidence building. "I know it just eats you up that you have years of seniority on me, and yet, you have to answer to me. You just need to resign yourself to the fact that I am in charge of this laboratory."

Doctor Brewer's face was on fire. Anger was swelling like a raging volcano about to explode. He removed the glasses from him mouth and placed them in the pocket of his white lab coat. He dropped his hands to his side and clinched his fists.

"Get over yourself, Doctor Brewer. You're jealous of the fact that science is passing you by and that I am on the verge of a major medical breakthrough. It kills you that it's top secret and you don't have access to it. It eats at you that you tried and couldn't do it and you're not in the limelight. It's killing you that…"

"Shut up, you little bitch!" he loudly interrupted. "I would slap you down, if it wouldn't cost me my job!"

Leah's eyes went wide and a lump swelled in her throat. She had let he anger electrify her words. Doug Brewer was a large man. He could snap her like a twig, if he wanted to. She was feisty but was it worth the risk. She would be no match for his extra-large frame. He wasn't muscular. In fact, he was fat. But there had to be a lot of muscle under his beefy exterior somewhere. In any event, he was intimidating.

She instantly retreated. His reaction took her by surprise. Sure, her tone was harsh, but, somehow, she expected him to stand there and take it. He lunged toward her. She back peddled until he had her pinned against the wall.

"Let me tell YOU something," his deep, booming voice sounded. His shoved a finger at her until it was a mere inch from her nose. "This used to by MY laboratory until you came along. Hell, as far as I'm concerned, it still is. You may be considered the boss," he said while drawing quotations in the air on boss, "but I run this laboratory and you damn well better figure it out before you get yourself in some trouble you won't want."

Leah's face was stinging. It was true she held the title of supervisor of the research laboratory. It was also true she was the lead scientist on the stem cell project, but Doug Brewer had tenure. It was grandfathered in the contract when she was promoted to the position. She could not fire or dismiss him without a higher authority. Her only recourse was to have him brought up before the board. And, it was only an option if there was physical violence, sexual harassment, or tampering with scientific data.

"Even when there's negativity brought toward our research, you get the limelight!" he snarled, pointing to the newspaper. "Well, I'm sick of it! If it's the last thing I do, I will regain my laboratory, Miss Stone. You can count on that. And you're little bitch ass will be gone!"

Chapter 18

Max and John entered the double glass doors to the forensic lab. They were promptly greeted by Terry Green.

"Good morning, gentlemen," he said as he shook their hands. "I've been waiting for you."

"Captain Lee said you had news for us," Max said.

"Yes, follow me, gentlemen." He motioned as he turned.

The two detectives followed him to his office. It was a smaller, glass-encased lab, smack in the middle of the main laboratory. His office was spotless and smelled of Lysol. A stainless steel table ran the length of the right hand side of the room. Everything on the table had been perfectly placed, including a microscope and a collection of other sophisticated equipment. Terry sat behind a desk comprised of a glass table top with chrome legs and invited them to sit. Behind his desk were glass and chrome bookshelves, filled to capacity with various books and periodicals.

"Now," he said as the two detectives sat, "let me show you what we found."

He opened a manila folder that had been placed on the corner of his desk. He turned it, making it was legible to the detectives. "We found hair samples, pulled from her clothes that matched Nathan Anderson. Additionally, we were able to match hair samples, found on the clothes you seized at his apartment, to Misty Lawrence."

"So far, so good," Max acknowledged. "But, no offense, Terry, that doesn't really prove much. We already know they were together and intimate. Matching hair samples doesn't prove he killed her. It just proves they were together. Tell us about the blood samples you mentioned to Captain Lee."

Terry held up a palm. "I'm getting to that. Just hold your horses," he chuckled. "We took skin samples from under Misty's fingernails and found it to match our suspect."

"Really?" Max questioned. "Now that does thicken the plot."

"Yes," Terry acknowledged. "Also, a blood splatter analysis showed Nathan Anderson's blood on the clothes we found near the victim. And, as Captain Lee told you, we found blood samples that matched the D.N.A. of the victim, on the clothes you obtained from the suspect's apartment.

John looked at his partner. "That's enough for a probable cause hearing and certainly enough to go ahead and hold him."

Max agreed.

"Any semen?" Max asked.

"Yes, and the D.N.A. showed it matches the suspect. But, knowing they were intimate doesn't prove much either."

"Unless the sex with him wasn't consensual," John said.

"Oh, come on, Tank. According to her parents they had been together for a while. Trust me, they were having sex, and probably lots of it," Max said.

"No, no, I'm not a dumbass. I mean what if it wasn't consensual this time. Remember, they did leave the bar in a heated argument. I doubt she would give it up willingly under the circumstances."

"Well, there's some truth to that, but knowing they were having consensual sex, you would never be able to convince a judge or jury that this time was different. The only witness that could refute it is dead and, besides that, Nathan Anderson has more to worry about than rape." Max thought for a moment and shook his head. He refocused his attention to Terry. "Terry, the girl's ovaries were cut out." Terry nodded his head as he listened closely. "And, of course the note," he paused. "We think a possible motive, besides out of pure anger, was that Misty might be pregnant and Nathan was making sure she didn't have the baby."

Terry shook his head. "Sorry, Max, she wasn't pregnant."

Chapter 19

"Well, well, well," Max said in a lofty smart-assed tone. "How the hell are your accommodations, Mr. Anderson?" He placed his hands on the black iron bars and shook them.

He was sitting alone on a small metal framed cot in a dimly lit cell. He wore the unmistakable orange jail colors. The walls were concrete and damp. The toilet was rust-stained, missing the seat, and smelled of decaying fecal matter. Next to it was a small sink that also had the appearance of years of neglect. Rust stains formed a copper colored streak from the constant drip of the faucet.

"Go get screwed!" he said without getting up.

"You know," John smirked, "if that's what you really want, we can arrange that for you. After all, this is jail. I'm sure we can find you a willing partner."

Nathan realized that defiance and anger wasn't going to get him anywhere. He would try a something different. He stood and approached the black iron bars. "Detective Stone," he said calmly, "someday soon you will learn that I am innocent of the charges. I know you don't believe me, but I would never hurt Misty." He paused for a moment. "I loved her and still do."

"You might have loved her," Max didn't doubt him. "You might find it interesting to know that many homicides are committed in the name of love, Mr. Anderson."

"But I didn't do it!" he replied frantically.

"Yeah, well, I guess a judge and jury will decide if that is true or not, huh?" The truth is, Nathan," he said as he leaned close to the bars, "I think you're a pretty good guy. I just think you have a temper and you lost yours when your girlfriend embarrassed you in front of a crowd.

"But I didn't kill Misty! I swear!" he said, clutching the bars. "I didn't kill her," he said, letting the words drift to silence.

"Wow, what a performance," Max mocked as he looked at his partner.

"Yeah, almost worthy of an academy award," John agreed.

"You guys are so amused with yourselves," Nathan said. "Well you two can go screw each other!"

"You know it's that type of foul vaginitis of the mouth that put you here," Max said.

"Tell me, Detective Stone," he pleaded. "Why don't you believe me? What makes you think I killed her? An argument in a bar doesn't make me a killer."

"I'm sure your attorney will point all of that out to you when he comes to see you, but…"

"No," he interrupted. "I'm asking you. What makes you think I did this?" he asked again.

"You do understand you have the right to remain silent? Do you really want to talk to us right now?"

"Yes, of course. I have nothing to hide."

"Very well, then. One word, evidence." Max was blunt.

"Evidence? What evidence?" he asked. "You've got no evidence on me because I didn't do anything."

"Let's start with Misty's hair samples pulled from your clothes and hair samples pulled from her clothes that belonged to you."

"So what? I don't deny we were together." He paused as he realized what the detective was saying. "And what do you mean my clothes?"

"We have the clothes you were wearing, Mr. Anderson. And they told us plenty," Max said with confidence.

"How did you get my clothes?"

"Now you knew the answer to that question before you even asked. Now, should I go on?"

Nathan didn't say a word.

"The lab was also able to obtain blood splatters on your clothes that matched Misty's D.N.A."

"But, I can explain that. I had Misty by the arm, I don't deny that. But, when we got outside she managed to pull her arm free and, in doing so, I accidentally scratched her arm. She got pissed and wiped the blood from her arm on my shirt.

"Well, hell then, that explains it all," Max mocked. "I should just go ask them to let you out right now."

"I know you don't believe me and I don't care."

"How do you explain your skin cells beneath her fingernails?" Max asked.

"I would guess from the same thing. When I scratched her arm, she got mad and scratched me back on purpose. See?" He showed the scratches on his right arm.

"All that proves is that you and she had a struggle. Those scratches could have been because she was fighting for her life," John said.

"You'll see! It will all come out in court, you'll see!" He was defiant.

Chapter 20

"How was work today, baby," Leah asked as Max entered the bedroom.

She had just stepped from the shower and was running a towel through her blond hair to dry it. He watched her sway and jiggle in all the right places. Her body glistened from droplets of water. The image aroused him.

"Not bad," he said as he took *"Raven"* from his shoulder holster and placed it on his nightstand. He sat on the bed and began to take off his shoes. He was damn glad to be home.

"How was your day?" he asked as his second shoe clunked to the floor.

"Mine sucked," she snickered as she sat on the opposite side of the bed.

She began rubbing lotion on her legs. The aroma of cherry blossom filled the room and met his nose. This alluring scent was Max's favorite. He took in a deep breath and sighed with his exhale.

Leah laughed as he pretended to be in a trance over the intoxicating smell.

"Uh, honey? We were talking about my shitty day," she reminded him.

"Oh, yeah," he joked. "What made your day so bad?"

"I got into an argument today with that prick Doug Brewer." She felt a little anger surge with just the mention of his name.

"Why?"

She swung her legs up onto the bed to turn and face him. "Because the bastard is jealous of me. Can you believe that? He actually got in my face today, pissing and moaning because the newspaper interviewed me."

"I read the article this morning," he replied. "It was good."

"I know, honey, but it pissed him off. He's jealous of my accomplishments. Why does he have to be that way?" she questioned with teary eyes.

Max didn't have time to respond.

"You know, why can't people just be happy with the fact that I'm using the talents God gave me for the betterment of the world? I'm on the verge of something so big the world doesn't even know how it can change humanity."

Max leaned back across the bed and pulled her to him. He wrapped his around her. Her skin was still warm from her typical hot shower and still, somewhat damp. He felt the erect nipples of her heavy breast press against his chest and it instantly placed erotic thoughts in his head. *"Now was not the time,"* he thought to himself. It was unlike her to get so upset so easily. She was usually a tough-as-nails chick and rarely allowed herself to be exposed this way, especially over a person that meant nothing to her. She was extremely passionate about her profession and, being considered among the best in the world, placed extra pressure on herself. She handled the pressure of her profession with grace and dignity. And, she was able to handle the negative pressure of those against it and what she stood for.

Max patted her lower back. "It's ok, baby girl if he can't..."

Suddenly, Leah raised her head from his chest and sat up. "Of course it's ok" she said.

Max couldn't hide the surprise on his face. He thought she was quite upset and suddenly the tough chick he knew appeared before his eyes.

"That bastard can kiss my ass."

"There's my baby." Max encouraged.

Her tears were replaced with hunger and desire as the gold flakes in her chestnut colored eyes seemed to sparkle. In a flash, she had grabbed him by the wrists, forced him onto his back, and sat upright on top of him. Her face showed the jubilance of that of a wrestler pinning his opponent. Then, her playful smile turned to a sultry, seductive pout.

Max and Leah spent the next hour in a passionate love making session. When they were done, they were spent.

They lay, holding each-other, and allowed things to return to normal. After several minutes of silence, they did.

"Honey?" Leah said softly as if it were a question.

"Yeah?"

"I didn't know if I should say or not, but I knew that girl." Her voice was sad.

"Who? What girl?" He was confused.

"I didn't realize it until I read the paper this morning."

"What girl?" Max asked again.

She braced herself up on her elbow, "Misty Lawrence."

Chapter 21

"What?" Max exclaimed.

"Well, I didn't know her, know her," she explained, "but she was in the seminar that I did at the campus and I talked to her."

Max said nothing but his eyes told her to tell him more.

"I didn't realize it until I read the paper today." She felt empathy as she wiped a tear. "I just think it's a terrible, terrible thing to happen to anybody, especially a young person who has their whole life ahead of them."

The natural buzz of lovemaking quickly faded away.

"You realize how she died?" He asked her.

"Yes," she replied soberly. "It's so sad."

The wheels were turning in Max's head. Thoughts raced through his brain like race cars when the green flag dropped. He already knew Misty Lawrence's ovaries and fallopian tubes were taken. He also knew a note was left, boasting the murderer needed those items more than Misty did. He was working with the theory Nathan Anderson had done it to prevent an unwanted pregnancy. That was disproven. According to lab results, she wasn't pregnant. Still, he could have killed her out or rage or, perhaps, she was cheating. If that were the case, why not just kill her? Why would he take reproductive organs? That made no sense to him. Did Nathan even have the knowledge to know where and how to remove them? Max had pretty much evaluated him as a womanizing bum. Perhaps he wasn't their man. No, the evidence fingering him was overwhelming. He deleted the idea as quickly as it entered his thoughts.

Still, there were the phone calls declaring Leah as a target. He was working under the assumption the two were not connected. Now, with the knowledge Misty was at Leah's seminar, he wasn't sure.

The killer had told him more than he intended when he phoned Max at the restaurant. His intentions were to taunt him and let him know he was watching them. But, he bragged about killing Misty. When he called Max during dinner, the news had not yet reached the media. There was no other way he could have known. The big question was could that person be Nathan Anderson?

Yes, it could be, but why? He had motive, he had opportunity, he had no alibi, he had a temper, and there was mounting forensic evidence against him. There was even Celeste Schneider. The stupid shit people do in the name of physical attraction to the opposite sex.

It could have been Nathan, he supposed, tossing out false clues in hopes of throwing him off. Was he that smart? If so, how did Leah fit into the picture? She hadn't done a damn thing to Nathan Anderson.

But Max had. Max had been to his apartment earlier in the evening and, for all practical purposes, forced his way in by threatening his roommate. His roommate could have tipped him off. Max was building a case against him for murder. What better way to get even?

When Max received the first call, he didn't know who the hell Nathan Anderson was. But, could Nathan Anderson have known who he was? Possibly. Since Nathan and Misty was an item, he would have been aware of the seminar that Misty had attended. And, since he would have known that, it is likely he would have known who Leah Stone was. It could be a connection. Perhaps he is against the research but Misty was for it. Is that why her ovaries and fallopian tubes were taken?

Max finally broke his thoughts. "You talked to her at your seminar?"

"Yes. She seemed like a very sweet girl."

"And you know her reproductive organs were stolen when she was murdered?"

She swallowed hard. "Yes."

"Can you think of any reason why someone would cut out the ovaries and fallopian tubes of a woman?"

"No, not really, other than possibly a surgeon during a hysterectomy."

"No, no. Why would a killer want them?

"I don't know. The ovaries only have two primary functions, the production of eggs and the production of hormones. Once removed, they are, pretty much useless." She paused for a moment. "Wait, I have heard of a relatively new procedure where women can get ovary transplants."

"What? What is that supposed to do?"

"Well, there was a procedure done where they transplanted ovaries in mice and it extended their life by more than forty percent and they think it could work in women."

"Really?" Max was stunned.

"Scientists also think it could restore fertility in older women, allowing them to have children later in life."

"That's insane."

He wondered if he was dealing with something he hadn't thought about. He had heard of illegal organ trafficking, mostly in foreign countries, but here?

"Oh my God, honey, I just thought of something."

"What?"

"I remember, she approached me after the seminar and asked me how she could donate eggs."

Chapter 22

The next few days flew by for Max. Each day, he proceeded with his usual morning routine. He would fill his cup with fresh hot coffee, pick up the morning paper and make his way to his desk.

He and John had spent a great deal of time working with Brandon Seymour from the district attorney's office. He was a hard charging, young, energetic attorney. Many had said he was an up-an-coming star. When it came to the law, Brandon was as sharp as they came.

During their meetings, they covered forensic evidence and testimony they would need to secure probable cause verdicts on Nathan Anderson and Celeste Schneider. The hearings were scheduled for today at 11:00 a.m.

The two detectives, along with the attorney, entered the courtroom through large wooden double doors.

A few moments later, the bailiff's voice brought the court to attention as the judge appeared through a door adjacent to his towering bench. The buzzing of chit-chat stopped and the sound of thirty or so people rising from their chairs filled the air, followed by silence again.

He stepped up behind his desk, paused as he surveyed the room, and permitted the room to sit as he positioned himself behind his desk.

Over the next thirty minutes, Brandon Seymour called Max and then John, building his case against Nathan Anderson on the charge of first degree murder and Celeste Schneider on the charge of accessory to murder and aiding and abetting a suspected felon.

Max told the court what he had witnessed and had uncovered in his investigation. When he was finished, Detective John Thompson gave his account of facts and findings. The prosecutor introduced D.N.A. samples and other forensic evidence linking Nathan Anderson to the death of Misty Lawrence.

Sufficient evidence was found to bind them both over for trial. Bail was denied for Nathan, but Celeste was allowed to bond out.

The two were pleading and arguing with their attorney as they were led from the court room.

Max's phone vibrated. A quick glance showed it was Peggy Meece. "What's up Peggy?"

"Max, can we meet? I need to talk to you. It's important."

Chapter 23

Tears stained Kaliana Sun's face. She feared she was about to die. Only an hour ago, she was working and dancing. Now, her life was in danger.

She didn't see her captor's face. He approached her as silent as a ghost and placed a chloroform-laced towel over her mouth and nose. She was out in seconds.

She had no idea how long she had been unconscious, where she was, or what he wanted with her. Hell, she didn't know, and didn't understand, anything that was going on. What the hell did he want, anyway? Her brain was pleading with her to struggle and get away, but her body would not cooperate. She kept slipping between awareness and unconsciousness. Everything was confused and jumbled in her brain. She tried to swallow, but couldn't. She tried to reason, but no words would escape her lips. All she could do was watch and obey as he threw her to the ground and tied her up.

He worked quickly, diligently, and with purpose. He sat across her abdomen as she lay flat on the ground. He pulled a dog chain anchor from a duffle bag and sunk it in the ground just beyond the fingertips of her right arm. Once he was satisfied it was secure, he retrieved some strong, thin nylon rope and tied her right wrist to the anchor. He quickly did the same on her left side. Turning his back to her face, he did the same with her feet, forcing her legs apart as far as he could. When he was finished, she was tightly bound to the ground with her arms stretched out and her legs spread eagle, with all four limbs anchored to the ground. He stood up, surveyed his work and nodded his head in satisfaction as a grin crept across his evil face.

The effects of the chloroform were starting to wear off and she could focus a little through her puffy and swollen eyes.

"What do you want with me?" she said, trembling with fear.

"You will not speak unless I speak to you," he said with a deep and dominate voice. He pointed a black-gloved finger at her from his towering position over her body. "If you scream, you will die! Understand?"

She nodded. Her tears were hot as they dripped down her cheeks, leaving a black trail from her mascara. Her eyes were wide and hollow as she watched every move he made. Why wouldn't he answer her? If only she knew, maybe she could reason with him. She watched as he pulled the dark green duffle bag closer. He dug around in the bag for a moment and pulled something out. Her eyes caught a flash of silver from the blade of a large knife. She felt the blood draining from her face as she fought the urge to faint. She was nearly hyperventilating.

"Please sir," she stuttered with trembling lips, "please don't hurt me. I will do anything you want."

"Oh, you will do exactly what I want, little lady," he said coldly. He brought his bedraggled face within an inch of hers. "Make no mistake about that."

His breath smelled like he had brushed his teeth with bourbon.

"Please don't hurt me," she cried, now close to hysterics.

He brought the weapon to her throat. She swallowed hard. Her eyes were fixed on the cold steel blade. No matter how much she wanted to look away, she couldn't.

"I thought I told you to be silent," he said with a low tone. "Another word and I will...," he let his thought drift off as he moved the tip of the blade to her tender cheek.

She knew it was pointless. She reasoned, if she did behave he would let her live. Perhaps it was a sexual thing. "Yes, sir," she said softly as her lips trembled. "Just please don't hurt me," she said as calmly as she could.

He removed the weapon from her cheek, shoved it into the frozen ground beside her, and fumbled around in his bag once again.

She let her eyes fix on the trees above her head. The dark crooked branches had long since lost their foliage in the November weather. They reached toward the stars that dotted the cold night sky like boney, contorted fingers. She exhaled deeply, trying to remain calm, and noticed her breath escape her lips, like a ghost, in the crisp air. The cold ground below her had penetrated her clothes and made her skin so cold it stung. She turned her head and noticed she was next to a river. Oh my God! Was he going to drown her? Maybe he was going to rape her and dump her body in the frigid water. Oh God! The thought made her shudder. Her composure abandoned her once again. A thousand thoughts raced through her mind, all frightening.

Suddenly, the faint light of a shooting star caught her attention as it briefly lit up the eastern sky then disappeared. She closed her eyes and made a wish that she would get out of this somehow. Perhaps the bastard would just fall over and die! She prayed someone would come along and save her. Anything!

The stranger finished fumbling around in the duffle bag. Kaliana watched as he placed a piece of paper inside a small plastic baggie. It looked like a sandwich bag with a zip top on it. He placed it on the ground near her waist. He removed his gloves and began to unbutton her red, shiny shirt. She gasped as the cold air touched her exposed skin. She closed her eyes tightly as the felt his dirty hands work their way down the buttons. The thought of rape crossed her mind again and she trembled.

When he finished, he pushed the shirt down to her sides, exposing her red satin bra. He paused, watching her belly move up and down with the rhythm of her breathing. The look on his face showed his approval of her body. He allowed a dirty hand to slide across her breast and down her belly, tracing a small circle around her navel as if he were trying to seduce her. After a moment, he moved to her waist, unbuttoned her pants, and slid the zipper down. With one quick motion, he yanked her jeans and panties down as far as her spread legs would allow.

"Shaven?" he questioned. "How nice," he said with approval.

For the first time, Kaliana thought she might survive this. He seemed to be after her body. Perhaps if she cooperated he would just leave her here when he was done. Hopefully, someone would come along and find her before she froze to death.

He retrieved the knife near her head, cut off her jeans and panties, and tossed them to the ground. The rush of cold air striking her body made her gasp. He looked at her sternly.

"I'm sorry, sir," she muttered quietly. "It was just the cold air."

Her apology landed on deaf ears. He removed a thick, white strip of cloth and, without saying a word, tied it around her mouth. He turned his attention back to his work. She hoped it would be over soon.

She shook violently. Once finished, the stranger sat by her side and watched her, satisfied with his work. He was in no hurry.

She wondered what he was waiting for. It was driving her insane. Why didn't he just do it and get it over with? Finally, he spoke.

"Do you know why you are here?" his asked in a low, sandpapered voice.

She shook her head.

"Well, Kaliana, you should be mindful of the choices you make in life."

Shit! He knew her name! How the hell did he know that? She didn't remember him going through her purse. Maybe while she was out?

"Kaliana," he leaned closer to her ear, "you should be careful of what lists your name appears on."

Her eyes showed confusion. She honestly had no idea what he was talking about. She was just a college student for Christ's sake. She was barely twenty-one. Sure, she made the dean's list, but what would that have to do with anything?

"You're a Biology student?" he asked.

She nodded as she whimpered beneath the gag across her mouth.

"Well, Miss Sun, you're here because of a lecture you attended."

Again, she shook her head.

"You should be careful what meetings you like to attend."

She denied it.

He became angry. "Let me refresh your memory, you bitch," he spat. "You attended a lecture with a Doctor Stone about stem cell research. In fact," he continued, "you not only attended, you signed up to donate eggs." He finished by spitting in her face.

He was right. She believed in stem cell research. She, herself, had aspirations of becoming a scientist and doing research in the field like Leah Stone. Oh, why was this happening to her? She felt the need to vomit, but fought the urge.

"Now that we have established you are a lying bitch..." he let his voice trail off to mumbling as he gathered his thoughts. "Nothing personal," he said, "but you should be careful of the people you associate yourself with, the meetings you attend, and what you volunteer for."

He turned and reached into his duffle bag to retrieve a surgical knife. "You see, dear one, Doctor Stone is trying to revolutionize the world and I don't like it. It must be stopped!"

Kaliana's face grew disfigured with terror. Her breathing was quick and shallow.

The stranger moved and positioned himself on his knees and between her legs. Moonlight glinted from the silver knife as he placed its cold blade on the right side of her torso. "You want to donate eggs?" He said with angry eyes turning red. "I will take your eggs so you can't!"

He applied pressure and slowly began to pull the knife toward him. She felt the knife sink into her flesh and a gush of warm blood instantly trickled down her side. Excruciating pain shot through her body. She was frantic now. She struggled against her restraints, but couldn't move. She screamed as loud as she could, but they were barely audible beneath her gag. The pain overwhelmed her senses. He watched her skin pull apart from the incision and was pleased. She fought for all she was worth. *"Please, God, help me,"* she kept repeating in her brain.

The stranger continued pulling the blade in a slight arc, following the contour of her body. He stopped just above her pelvic bone in the middle of her torso, about three inches below her belly button.

She was consumed with pain and her continued screams exploded inside her head. She fought as darkness teased her. He pulled the incision apart and his filthy fingers disappeared briefly inside her abdominal cavity. They returned bloody. He moved to her left side and repeated his repulsive actions.

Kaliana felt her life-blood draining from her body. Darkness continued to beckon her. Her pupils were dilated and she could hear her heart pound in her eardrums. She decided that screaming wasn't doing any good. She was too tired anyway. She must save her strength. Maybe someone would save her, but hope was escaping. She felt the weight of his body ease and she managed to focus long enough to see him crawl to her side.

"You won't need these." He chuckled in his deep voice as he showed her some of her own body parts like they were a prize. She vomited in her gag and was forced to swallow it.

It seemed funny to her that the pain wasn't all that bad now. The warmth of the blood on her backside was soothing. Amazingly, she felt a calming sensation wash over her.

He picked up the plastic bag that held the piece of paper and showed it to her. "You see this?"

She didn't respond to his question but he could hear, what sounded like, her talking to herself.

"Are we praying?" he mocked. "Go on, it won't help you. No one can help you." He got in her face. "You will die!"

She managed to look toward her stomach, but wished she hadn't. Her intestines were oozing from her incisions and her blood was bright crimson on her belly. She puked inside her gag again.

He shook the plastic bag at her. "This bag has a note in it for the one who finds you." He crawled to position his mouth near her ear and spoke softly. "I must ensure someone finds it, so I'm going to pin it to your belly button."

He moved to her side, pulled a safety pin from his pocket, and pierced the skin above her navel as he attached the note. She made no sound nor moved.

The stranger sat beside her and watched her eyes turn hollow and distant. The night became dark as death and summoned her. A moment later, Kaliana Sun gave in to its desire.

Chapter 24

"Max?" an excited voice echoed down the hall.

He and John looked up to see an animated Captain Lee rapidly approaching. Distress was on his face.

"Max," he said again, "we have a big problem."

"What is it, Captain?"

"I just took a call. You two have to go." Sadness crossed his aged face. "Max," his voice softened, "they found another girl."

"Another one?"

"I'm afraid so. Apparently she was killed like Misty Lawrence was. They found her in Broad Ripple Park." Captain Lee shook his head in disbelief. "You two better get up there."

"Right away, Captain." Max gulped the last bit of his coffee, slammed his cup down, and turned to his partner. "It's going to be one of those days."

They raced to Broad Ripple Park. It was located on the north central part of the city near the trendy little community of Broad Ripple. It was well known throughout the city as a place where the younger crowd loved to go bar hopping and partying. One could park and find better than thirty night clubs, bars, and comedy clubs well within walking distance.

The park, itself, was located just east of the main strip. On just about any given warm day, the park would be steep with activity, but in the winter, it was pretty much barren.

They parked the car next to the familiar white van with the black letters indicating it was from the Coroner's Office. The icy air stung their faces as they got out of the car. Max cinched up his leather coat and shivered briefly. He looked over at John, who was blowing hot air into his cupped hands.

Max hadn't noticed that Peggy Meece was sitting in the van until he heard the driver's door open. She was well dressed for the cold. Her coat, which was satiny pink in color with white faux fur around the hood, waist, and arms, covered her petite frame. She opted for white fuzzy earmuffs and allowed the hood to dangle on her back. The earmuffs allowed her reddish blond hair to shine in the sunlight. Her blue jeans where tight against her slender frame and the pant-legs were tucked inside of her furry, tan colored boots, which came halfway up on her calves. Her tanned face had an angelic look to it and her makeup was impeccable and highlighted her cute freckles. Her green emerald eyes almost sparkled. The cold air instantly made her cheeks rosy.

"Hello, Miss Meece," Max said as he reached for her hand.

"Hi, Max," she brimmed with a bright smile. Her teeth were perfectly straight and brilliantly white. "Good morning, John," she said, looking in his direction.

"Good morning, Peggy," he said warmly.

Max gave her a quick look over. God, she was desirable. He could not figure out how someone so perky and full of life could ever work around so much death and destruction. Her reaction to what was going on around her was the exact opposite he had witnessed just a few days ago when she was with them at the murder scene of Misty Lawrence. She was so distressed then and nearly had a breakdown. It was obvious she didn't know the details surrounding this murder.

"Forgive me, Peggy, but you do not look like you're dressed for a murder investigation," Max said.

Her eyes lowered. "Actually, no," she apologized. "I was supposed to be off today but got called in. If you remember, Max, we were supposed to meet today at Starbucks."

Her bubbly personality made her come across as quite flirty. She was sexy in every sense of the word. Peggy didn't know that and was unspoiled. To Max, that made her all the more attractive.

"I remember, but circumstances had other ideas for us." He smiled warmly. "We'll have to reschedule it."

"Those officers told me you two were coming so I thought I would just wait where it was warm. Not much I could do until you got here anyway," she said.

"You haven't been to the scene?" Max asked.

"No, why?" she asked as an expression of concern crept across her face.

Max moved close enough to her to put his hands on her shoulders. He got a whiff of her perfume. The aroma was seductive. "It's my understanding this homicide is patterned like the one we worked together a few days ago," Max said calmly.

"Oh, God!" her voice trembled as her leather-gloved hands covered her gasping mouth. "That poor girl." she wept.

Max pulled her close to comfort her. He patted her back. "Peggy," he said as he pushed back from her, "why don't you get someone else down here to work this one?"

"No, I'll be ok."

Max wasn't sure if she was trying to reassure him or herself. "Are you sure?"

"Yes. I have to do my job." She forced a smile.

"Ok, then, let's go do what we're paid to do."

"Yeah, I don't get paid enough for this part," John said.

The three made their way to a group of disinterested police officers huddled in a circle near the edge of a sidewalk. It appeared to be a starting point for a paved walking path at the foot of the woods.

Max could hear the three officers laughing and cutting up as he approached, but couldn't make out what they were talking about. Their jovial attitude and lack of professionalism angered him. John could tell his partner was agitated.

"Let it go, Max," he said as he nudged his arm. "We have more important things to do right now."

"Good morning, Detective Stone," one of the officers said cheerfully as they passed.

Max knew his partner was right. He merely nodded his head
in recognition toward the three officers as he passed.

"Detective Stone?" one of the officers said.

Max stopped and turned to face them. "What?"

"Just go down the sidewalk about a quarter mile and make a left toward the river. You'll find forensics near the scene."

Max flatly thanked them and turned back to follow the sidewalk with John and Peggy.

They covered the quarter mile and turned left on another sidewalk. It was a swift downhill hike that wound around a wooded area made up mostly of sycamore, cottonwood, and red and silver maple trees, all beautiful and shady in the summer, but barren and lifeless in the winter.

The crime scene was near the river, just at the edge of the tree line. They found Terry Green, and another forensic specialist, carefully sweeping the scene. Two other officers were securing the area with crime-scene tape.

Terry looked up and acknowledged the three as they approached. "Good morning, Max, John, Peggy," he said as he shook each ones hand.

"Morning, Terry," was said in succession by each.

"Goddamn," Max spat as he looked at the body of the victim.

She was anchored to the ground like the last victim. She was young, beautiful, and Asian. Her clothes had been ripped from her body and she was totally nude. Her tender, slim abdomen had been sliced down each side to her pelvis and her vagina had been abused as well. Trickles of dried blood showed the path down her sides and stained the ground around her a deep brick red. Her once olive colored skin was pale and had a blue tinge. Her almond shaped eyes were slightly open and lifeless and her waist length black hair was mussed up around her head.

"I will get the sick bastard that is doing this!" Max vowed. Movement caught the corner of his eye and he turned to watch Peggy run to the edge of the tree line and vomit. "Poor girl," he said softly.

"I'll go take care of her, Stoney." John said as he patted Max on the back. "You do what you need here."

Max acknowledged and John went to comfort her.

"She's not cut out for this," Terry said after John left.

"Naw, it doesn't suit her personality. But, seeing another woman like this has to be especially hard on her," Max answered.

He sighed and squatted next to the body of the young girl, "What do we know about her, Terry?"

Terry squatted next to the detective, "Well, just like the last time, her ovaries and fallopian tubes appear to have been taken and her uterus was bludgeoned. The perpetrator also left pinned a note to her navel, as you can see."

"Say the same thing as the last one?" Max asked.

"Yes." Terry shook his head as he picked up a small stick and began doodling in the dirt.

A few moments of silence passed. "Do we know her name?" Max finally asked, breaking the silence.

"Kaliana Sun," Terry replied flatly.

"Pretty name for a pretty lady," Max said as he pushed himself to a standing position.

"Yeah," Terry agreed as he followed suit and stood. "We found her purse near the body, complete with all her identification and about five-hundred dollars in cash, mostly singles.

"Whoever is doing this, isn't doing it for money," Max said.

"Nope."

"Anything else?"

"Yes, her I.D. shows she was twenty-one and enrolled at IUPUI. And, believe it or not, we found an un-cashed payroll check from Mr. Swellington's."

"She's a stripper?" Max was surprised.

"Was," Terry corrected. He handed Max a sheet of paper. "Here's all her information. Her parents have been notified, but they live in California."

"Thanks, Terry," Max said as he took the paper, folded it, and placed it in his coat pocket.

"Any witnesses?"

"It's early but so far nobody has come forward."

"Two murders and no witnesses. Terry," he exhaled, "we have a problem."

Terry nodded in agreement.

John approached Max. Terry dismissed himself and made his way over to the other forensic specialist.

"Looks like you and I get to go to the titty bar in a day or two," he said when John arrived.

"Well, that'll be different for me," John said. "I don't patronize those places." He grinned wryly.

Max knew his best friend was lying. He motioned toward Peggy. She was still squatting at the tree line with her head in her hands. "How's she doing?"

"She's pretty shook up. I really feel for her." His tone was sad. "She said she would like to talk with you, alone."

Max's eyebrows rose. "Why?"

"She's feeling pretty bad about what happened and wants to talk with you."

Max looked in her direction. She was now sitting on the ground with her back up against a Sycamore tree. Her head was down and her arms were draped over her knees.

John patted Max on the back. "I'll meet you in the car. I need to go call in another person from the Coroner's office to work this scene anyway. Take as much time as you need with Peggy."

He thanked his partner, quickly covered the forty yards to the tree line, and sat on the ground next to Peggy. Her mascara had mixed with salty tears and formed dark smudges under her eyes and on her cheeks.

"What can I do for you, Peggy?"

"Max, I can't do this anymore. I've decided to quit the Coroner's office."

Chapter 25

John was sitting in the driver's seat and had it reclined as far as it would allow. He was nearly asleep when he heard the passenger side car door open and Max got into the car. At the same time, the driver's door on the white van next to them opened and closed as Peggy got into her van.

"Well?" John asked. He returned his seat to the proper position.

"Well, what?" Max buckled his seat belt.

"You know damn well, what. What's up with Peggy? Don't hold out on me."

"Not here." Max motioned to the van. "Let's go."

John started the car, they waved at Peggy, and they headed toward headquarters.

"Ok, what's the scoop?" John asked again as soon as the car left the park.

"Not much to say, really. I think Peggy's done."

"Really?"

"This job doesn't suit her. You know that."

"Well, yeah, but what's that got to do with you?"

"I dunno," Max shrugged his shoulders. "Apparently she sees me as someone she can talk and relate to." He looked over at his partner. He had a smirk on his face. "What?"

"She wants your body," he teased.

"Get serious." Max chuckled.

"I am serious. You know all women want to dine at the all you can eat Max Stone buffet," he said as he nudged Max with his elbow.

"Well, not all women," Max joked. After a moment of silence, the mood turned serious again. "She told me she couldn't do it anymore and was going to resign."

"Wow, sounds serious."

"It is."

"Do you know how long she's been working for the Coroner's office?"

"Yeah, she told me about five months."

"That's not long."

"Well, if you ask me, it is five months too long for someone like her," Max said bluntly.

"What will she do, though?"

"She said she could go back to her old job, but she wouldn't tell me what. In fact, she said she could start tonight or tomorrow if she wanted. She said it paid great money, but the hours sucked."

"Yeah, second shift jobs suck."

"She wasn't sure she wanted to go back to that job either, but at least it would pay the bills and she wouldn't have to see death and destruction. She said it was actually a mostly fun job."

"What'd you tell her?"

"I told her all the death and destruction was hard on her and that I felt like it didn't suit her. I told her she should do some serious thinking."

"Good advice," John said.

"I don't know," Max shook his head. "I was supposed to meet her over a cup of coffee today. She told me that was what she wanted to talk to me about even before all this happened. She was already thinking she didn't want to do this anymore. I think the first murder really got to her and the second one finished her."

"You're a good man, Max Stone."

"Shit!"

"What, what is it?" John asked.

"It just struck me."

"What?"

"You do realize that Nathan Anderson and Celeste Schneider are innocent, or so it would seem."

"Yeah, you're right."

"We are going to have one pissed off son of a bitch."

"Well, let's get it over with."

They arrived at the jail. Nathan Anderson was sitting in his cell with his head lowered. He rose to his feet as he heard the footsteps echo down the hallway. His eyes became instant anger as the two detectives approached.

"I thought it smelled like shit in here," he said as they stopped at his cell.

"Just settle down, Nathan," John cautioned.

"Go to hell."

"Check your anger," Max said. "We actually have good news for you."

"Really?" He was sarcastic. "What kind of good news?"

"It pains me to say this, but we've discovered that you may actually be innocent and we will be letting you go."

A large smile crossed his face and turned to a gaping grin. "I told you assholes I was innocent. I should sue your asses. What made you finally believe me?"

"We found another victim that was killed like Misty," Max said.

Nathan's stance of defiance softened. "I'm very sorry to hear that." His thought of his dead girlfriend. "I hope you catch whoever is doing this."

"Anyway, we've already gone to Judge Fish to explain the circumstances and the paperwork for your release is being processed now. You should be out soon."

As if on cue, their conversation was interrupted by a jailer, who had come to release Nathan from his imprisonment. The sound of the lock tumblers echoed in the vacant hallway. The steel door swung open with a creek and he stepped from his dingy, dirty cell into bright florescent lamps that lined the ceiling of the hallway. He paused, took a deep breath, exhaled, and extended an open hand to Max. "No hard feelings, detective. Just bring Misty's killer to justice."

Chapter 26

A cold front had moved through during the night, which wasn't unusual for this time of year. With each front, the weather turned colder. Soon it would just stay cold and not get warm until the spring.

Most mornings Max would listen to blues on his way to the office, but this morning he lowered the volume and allowed his thoughts take him to work.

He had been in law enforcement since he was twenty-four. His profession had been chosen for him when he was just a boy when he awoke one morning to find his parents murdered in their bed. He knew from that day forward he wanted to be on the side of righteousness. He never understood why anybody would want to inflict intentional pain on someone. He didn't know why his parents had been murdered. Nor, why the murderer, or murderers, had spared his life. And, after all these years, why hadn't the murder been solved? This is what drove him most. This is what tore at his soul.

Any yet, for his years of investigative work, this current case gave him a feeling in the pit of his stomach that he hadn't felt since waking up as a boy and seeing his parents dead and bloody.

It was beginning to show signs of a serial killer. Already two young girls had been murdered. There was no real reason, as if there ever is. Why these two and why in this gruesome, ritualistic manner? There didn't seem to be any real connection. One was a typical Midwestern girl with a typical American family, and the other was of Asian descent and happened to be a stripper, with parents from the west coast. It would be hard, no impossible, to make it about race.

Max's thoughts returned to the murder scenes of both young ladies. They had been anchored to the ground. Yet, neither had been raped or sexually assaulted. So, the murders weren't sexually motivated. Their abdomens had been surgically cut along both sides and down to their vaginal area. What really puzzled Max was that their ovaries and fallopian tubes had been taken? The killer had not taken money or other items but did leave a note. Yes, the note. It said the killer needed them more than the victim.

But why? What the hell was all that about? Why would someone take a woman's reproductive organs? What use would it be to anybody?

He remembered Leah telling him about a new procedure called ovarian transplant. Could he really be dealing with organ harvesting? He had done some research since learning of the transplants and the potential benefits of having it done. The first successful transplant was done in India. Thieves were making big money from stealing everything from kidneys to eyeballs. Why not ovaries? It was possible. But, if it were true, why commit such a ritualistic killing?

So far, no real forensic evidence had been left at either scene so the bastard knew what he was doing. The only real clues were the note, the manner by which they were killed, and both were college students. Wait a minute. Yes, both were college students and both went to the same college. It wasn't much, but by-God it was something! And what about Leah? Apparently she was still in danger. He had once thought Nathan Anderson could have been the suspect, but that was looking less like a possibility since he was behind bars when the second murder happened.

Max cranked up the volume on the radio, and finished his morning commute to the precinct.

It was going to be a long day.

He grabbed a cup of coffee and sat at his desk to read the morning paper. He flipped it open to read the front-page headline: *Second Woman Found Dead.* His heart saddened as he was reminded of the murder of Kaliana Sun. He became angered and his heart pounded as he browsed over the article. Next, he browsed the sports page. By the time Max finished reading about his beloved

Colts dropping a close one to the Titans, his cell phone rang. He checked the caller I.D. and it read unknown.

"Hello, this is Max Stone," he said.

"Well, well, well," the voice said smugly. "Mister Stone, how are you this morning?" His voice was evil. "Have you seen the morning paper, Mister Stone?"

Max was seething. What he couldn't figure out was why this person thought it was funny to call and torment him. He wondered if it was the actual killer or was it someone's way of playing a sick joke by calling him whenever there was another murder. The calls seemed to be coming closer. And what the hell was it all about? This man maintained he was going to kill Max's wife, Leah. Max had no idea what this man's motivation or purpose was, or what connection Leah had to the murders, but he wanted to take him down and take him down hard.

"Yeah, I saw the paper, you sick son of a bitch." Max was angry.

"Shocking about young Kaliana, wouldn't you say Detective Stone?"

Max knew he was talking to the killer. The article in the paper did not give the victim's name, like before. Only the actual killer would know the name of the victims.

"Tell me, how all of this is connected to my wife?"

"Now, Detective Stone," he replied grimly, "do I really need to do your job for you and prove that I am right?" The mysterious voice paused for a moment. "Oh, by the way, Detective Stone, did you happen to notice that the second murder was closer to your home than the first?"

Shit! He was right. Was this by design? Would there be another one closer yet? Would this eventually lead to his very home? Did he plan to kill Leah there?

Max was furious "I will bring you down long before you get to my house, you sick bastard."

"Oh, Detective Stone," he laughed, "I can take Leah at any time but it's so much more fun this way." He chuckled. "Goodbye for now, Detective Stone, there is much work to be done."

The phone went silent before Max could say another word.

Chapter 27

"Morning, Max," John said as he approached.

Max nodded as he lowered his cup from his lips, "Morning partner." He smiled.

"How was your weekend?"

The two spent the next several minutes in idle chit-chat and catching up from the past few days. Max, Leah, John, and Shawn usually hung out on Saturday nights, but not this weekend. Shawn had a company Christmas party so they went to that. Max also filled him in on the phone call he had just received and his fear for Leah's life.

The investigation had been quiet over the weekend, thank God. Max really needed a few days without worry of police business. He thoroughly enjoyed spending time over the weekend with the family over dinner and a movie. His mind did wonder from time to time about the two young women who had been brutally murdered. Every time his cell phone rang he feared it was the precinct calling him in for yet another murder but this weekend was his own.

The call this morning had set Max off but one call that he did receive over the weekend, he was all too happy to share with John.

"I got a call from Peggy Meece on Saturday morning," Max said cheerfully.

A devilish grin swept across John's face. "I told you she wanted to dine at the Max Stone buffet." He paused briefly. "So tell me, Mr. Stone, did you have a threesome with Peggy and the misses?"

"Get serious," Max teased back as he flung the sports section of the paper at his friend. "She called to tell me that she resigned from the Coroner's office on Friday and was starting back at her old job that evening." Max took a sip of his coffee. "She seemed very excited and happy."

"Great!" John was happy. "What is she doing now?"

"She wouldn't say. All she said was that the pay was great and it was a happier environment for her."

"Well, good. Anything has got to be better for her than collecting dead bodies," John said.

Max agreed and moved on to the next subject.

He proceeded to tell John about his thoughts on both murders being college girls and that he wanted to go out to the college to talk with the Dean to see if they can dig anything up. He also asked if John was busy that evening because he thought they needed to go out to the strip club to see what they could dig up there on the murder of Kaliana Sun.

They drove to the college to meet with Craig Propst. He was the long-time Dean at the university and held a doctorate degree in Psychology from UNC. Max and John were greeted by his secretary and were quickly ushered into his office.

Dr. Propst unfolded his tall frame from behind his large oak desk and extended a hand as Max and John entered.

"Good morning, gentlemen." His voice was soothing, baritone.

Both detectives shook his hand and returned the greeting.

He motioned to two executive leather chairs across from his desk, "Gentlemen, please."

They took up a position across from the dean and made themselves comfortable.

"Now," he started as he lowered himself in his own chair, "as I understand it, two of our young co-eds have been murdered?"

"Yes, sir." Max produced pictures of Misty Lawrence and Kaliana Sun and slid them across the desk.

Doctor Propst examined the pictures and slid them back to Max. "Tragic," escaped his lips as he shook his head. "I'm sorry, I didn't know them personally. We have over fifteen-thousand students at this campus. I did, however, remember the names you told me on the phone and took the liberty to pull their records."

He reached for a manila folder on the corner of his desk and produced the current schedules and academic records of the two victims, and slid them across his polished desk to Max.

Max opened the folders and studied for a moment. His eyes focused on the two's academic schedule and made a mental note of how heavy of a load that each was taking. One thing that caught his eye almost immediately was that both girls were in the Biology school and both were specializing in Embryonic Stem Cell Research. He also noticed they were consistently on the Dean's list.

"Very intelligent young ladies," Max said as he closed the folders.

Doctor Propst sat back in his chair. "Yes, they were both gifted," he said as he allowed the fingers of his hands to tap each other's finger tips. "On paper, at least, they were model students."

"Can you think of anything or anybody that might want to harm these two girls," John asked.

"No, not at all, Detective," he replied. "As I said, they were model students. Their records were impeccable. No trouble at all."

"Dr. Propst," Max said. "I'd like your help in green-lighting a visit with their professors. I'd like an opportunity to talk with them as well.

"Absolutely. Whatever you need, you let me know."

"I need a copy of their schedules, their dorm, or," Max hesitated, "Hell, I need a copy of this," he said as he held up the two folders.

"You may have those," Dr. Propst said as he gestured with his hand. "These are copies that I have already made for you." He paused for a moment then rose from his chair as if to announce the end of the meeting. "If there is anything more you need, please feel free to contact me." He stepped from behind his desk.

Max and John were still sitting in their chairs. They shared a *WTF?* glance, then rose from their sitting position, shook the Dean's hand, and exited the office door. They had what they came for, a possible connection.

As soon as they reach the hall, Max turned to Tank. "I need to talk to Leah, and now."

Chapter 28

"What's up Stoney?" John asked as soon as they reached the car. He knew Max knew something.

"Didn't you catch it?"

John was puzzled.

Max quickly opened the manila folders and shoved the victim's scheduled at his partner. "Both of those girls were in the Embryonic Stem Cell program and, at one time, so was Leah." He hesitated to allow that to sink in. "And, Leah just gave a seminar on the subject just a couple of weeks ago."

"I didn't think of that! I guess that's why they pay you the big bucks."

"In fact," Max continued, "Leah told me the other night that she remembered Misty Lawrence being in her seminar."

"Really?"

"Yeah, but I didn't think much about it at the time.

I thought it was just a coincidence." Max paused for a moment. "But now, with two dead girls," he stopped to formulate additional thoughts, "and both at IUPUI, and both in the Biology department," he allowed his thoughts to trail.

"Yes," Tank agreed. "It's beginning to add up to too many coincidences."

"Yep," Max said. "Well, we do know that Misty Lawrence was at Leah's seminar but we don't know if Kaliana Sun was. So, it could be nothing, but, then again, it might be something." He whipped out his cell phone and dialed his wife's number. "Let's see if we can find out."

"Stoney Baby!" she said with delight as she answered her phone.

"Hey, honey. I have a question. Do you have a copy of attendees from your seminar a couple of weeks ago?"

"Yes, of course I do, why?"

Max wasn't sure there was a connection yet and he sure as hell didn't want to alarm her about these murders. He made it a practice to not discuss police matters with her. He felt it kept her desensitized to all the brutal and horrible things he actually saw. He didn't know how to proceed. She already knew that one girl from her seminar was murdered. If it turns out that Kaliana Sun's name was on that list, she might freak out.

"Well, you remember telling me about that one girl had attended your seminar?"

"Well, uh, yes," she finally said.

"Well," he said cautiously. "We need the list for the investigation," he lied as he tried to dance as lightly as he could.

"Oh, well," she sensed there was more, "sure. I'll bring it home with me tonight."

"Thanks honey. I don't really have time to talk right now. Please find it and bring it home with you ok? Oh," he added, "don't forget Tank and I have to go to the strip club after work tonight about the investigation."

"Yeah, yeah," she chuckled. "I'll see you when you get home."

She didn't see how a strip club equated to an investigation, but she knew her husband and she knew his best friend Tank. They went, sometimes, and that was perfectly alright with her.

John knew Max and knew him well. He knew from his actions there was something more on his mind than just these gruesome murders. He could tell something was eating at him.

"What's going on, my friend?" John was concerned.

Max looked at him with question.

"Come on," John encouraged, "something's going on that you're not telling me. I know you too well."

Max knew that John wanted more information about the phone calls and how they possibly connected the murders to Leah. The truth was, it was eating at him. It was time he talked.

"You mean you want me to tell you about the calls and the threats on Leah's life?"

"Yes, of course."

"Well, up until now I felt it was all about me. The voice keeps saying he intends to prove that I am not a good detective and that I can't protect my own wife. Now, for the first time," Max paused, "I believe it might be about Leah. In fact, the killings might be about Leah."

"That sounds crazy," John said.

"Get this. The murders were also planned to get closer to my house with each victim."

John's eyes shot wide. "You didn't tell me that!"

Chapter 29

Have you told Leah?" John questioned.

"Are you serious?" Max's said. "I can't. Do you know what that would do to her?"

"Yeah, I see your point."

John tried to turn the conversation more positive. "Well, we'll just have to catch this bastard before he kills again." He glanced down at his watch and then smiled at his partner. "What do you say we go grab some dinner and go look at pretty, naked girls?"

He managed to get a slight smile out of Max.

"You do realize that we are going as part of an investigation, don't you?"

"Uh, yes, of course." John smiled again and winked at him.

John swung the car into a Chili's and they ate dinner. After that, they got back in the car and made their way to Mr. Swellington's strip club.

The sound of loud, thumping music blasted their ear drums and the smell of various perfumes invaded their nostrils the moment they walked through the door. They paid the cover charge, strolled past the bouncer, and into the purple and pink neon light show of sin. The place vibrated with life to the loud music and was surprisingly busy for 6 p.m. Strippers, in various stages of nudity, were performing on three separate stages as the lights flashed all around.

"Let's find our man and get this over with," Tank said as he leaned close to Max's ear.

"What's your hurry?" Max chuckled. "Let's check out the ladies."

"I don't frequent places like this," He shouted over the music. "These places make me uncomfortable."

About the time he got the word uncomfortable out of his mouth, a beautiful hand with fire-engine red painted finger nails slipped over his shoulder from behind and caressed his cheek. An alluring, half-dressed woman positioned herself in front of him and put her arms around his neck. She had long, straight, straw colored hair and sparkling blue eyes. Her bountiful breasts were begging to spill over her shiny purple bikini top as she winked at him.

"Hi Tank," she said in an angelic voice. "Good to see you again."

Max took in the beauty of the stunning woman draped around his buddy's neck and then looked at his friend, "You are so full of shit. You never come here, huh?" He chuckled.

Tank was busted. "Well," he shrugged his shoulders as he gently removed the beautiful girl's arms from around his neck, "I've been here a couple of times I guess." He laughed. "But, Candy, here," he motioned to her, "is an exception."

"Well, I can see that," Max said as he looked her up and down again. "But, let's remember what we are here for."

"Well, you did say we had time to check out the ladies."

"That I did, my friend," he conceded, "but let's take care of business first."

Tank hugged Candy and told her that he would see her later. She placed a finger to her lips and kissed it. Then, she placed the finger to Tank's lips, pouted and waved at him, and dismissed herself. The two made their way to the bar.

"Well, hello gentlemen," came from the sultry voice attached to the sexy bartender, "I'm Angel. What'll be?" She winked.

Angel fit her well, Max thought. She was, in fact, angelic looking wearing a shiny pale pink teddy, complete with sparkling angel wings attached to the back of her costume. Her hair was brunette and highlighted with blond, long and straight. Her makeup was slight and her lips were full and pouty, shaded with cinnamon colored lipstick.

Max introduced himself and Tank and explained why they were there. She immediately led them toward the back of the building. They walked past the V.I.P. room where hot women, dressed in only G-strings, were gyrating and rubbing their asses on horny men sitting perfectly still, like stones, on leather couches. The men couldn't get their money out of their wallets fast enough to keep the ladies pushing their breasts against their cheeks and bottoms pulsating against their tightening jeans. To most of the men, these girls were a fantasy. Some figured if they spent enough money, an after-hour encounter might be in their future, but these girls were only in it for the money.

A few moments more, they arrived at the office of the club manager. He was a skinny twig of a black man. He looked like a skeleton wrapped in electrical tape. He had a sense of sleaze about him; the kind of man you could see selling sex dolls and dildos out of his garage.

He introduced himself as Marquis Booker and the three exchanged pleasantries. The smell of stale cigarette smoke distressed their nostrils as they entered the small, dirty office. His desk, which appeared to be as old as the paneling, was smallish, made of metal, and was painted beige. Max noticed several different colors from previous paint jobs showing in different areas of the scratched-up, dinged-up desk. On top of the desk, a desk calendar, complete with doodle marks, showed beneath scattered papers. On the corner of the desk, Max discovered the source of the foul air as he noticed an overflowing ash tray. A pack of Marlboros sat next to it. In the corner of the office stood a hunter green, five drawer filing cabinet that also bore the scars of years of punishment. A scratched tacky ceramic lamp, that was missing its shade, sat on top. It was the sole source of light. John's eyes were drawn to the floor as he watched a roach scurry under the filing cabinet and disappear. The sea foam green and white tiles were disgustingly dirty and severely worn.

As if out of instinct, he reached for the pack of Marlboro's on his desk, lit up a cigarette, took a puff, exhaled his putrid smoke, and placed it in the already full ashtray.

"Sorry, gentlemen," he apologized as he motioned to two plastic molded chairs in front of his desk. One was orange and the other was blue. "I only have enough room in the office for two chairs," he half-smiled. "I don't usually get more than one or two at a time in here anyway."

Max held his hands in protest. "That's ok, Mr. Booker. We won't be here very long."

Max was afraid to sit anyway.

"Very well," he conceded.

The meeting was brief and uninformative. He was, of course, familiar with Kaliana Sun, but her fans knew her by her stage name, Asia. She was one of the more popular girls at the Club. He didn't know about her murder until he was contacted about the meeting.

"She did not leave with anyone the night she was murdered," Marquis said. "Some of our girls do, in order to make a little extra money," he said with a sheepish grin, "but not Asia. She's a good kid. What the girls do outside these walls is none of my business."

"How do you know she left alone?" Max asked.

184

"Because I run a secure place here, Mr. Stone," he said curtly. "All," he paused, "I repeat, all of my girls are escorted to their cars at the end of their shift by my bouncers."

The three finished their meeting and Max and John stood, shook his hand, and excused themselves.

"Well, the works over," Max grunted playfully. "Let's have a drink and um," he cleared his throat and grinned, "stake things out."

John agreed and they went to the bar for a drink. Angel was still there.

"Well, hello again, gentlemen." She smiled at them. "You ready for that drink now?"

They sat at the bar and each ordered bourbon. They watched her prepare the drinks. Not terribly hard. Just pour some Jim Beam in a glass. Max smiled as he watched her as she prepared the drinks. She knew he was watching her. After all, wasn't she supposed to be flirty and make a man feel good about being a man? She reached for the bottle, strategically placed above her head. When she did, her teddy rode up to reveal her matching pale pink thong. She grabbed the bottle, smiled at them and pulled her teddy back down. As she sat the bottle on the counter, she placed her hand over her mouth and acted as if she were blushing. This act brought smiles to both as she poured and placed the drinks in front of them.

"Angel, huh?" Tank asked.

"Yes I am," she flirted.

"Well I don't know about Angel, but from what I see," he chuckled, "it sure looks like a piece of heaven to me."

She placed a hand on top of his. "Oh, you're so sweet."

Max grinned wide. It didn't surprise him about anything that came out of Tank's mouth. He knew the question was going to come. He just didn't know when.

"So," John continued as he took her hand in his, "you know we're detectives, right?"

"Yeah, sure," she said. "I like cops."

"Well, we're thinking we're going to have to arrest you for public indecency." He joked.

"And why is that, sir?" She played along.

"Well, Angel," he paused, "as you know we are in a strip club."

She nodded, trying to contain her amusement.

"And all these pretty girls are stripping for all the men in this joint."

She nodded again.

"And," he said, barely holding back his laughter, "here you are looking like," he paused, "well, an angel. So, when do we get to see the rest of you?"

And there it was; the question. John always liked to find out what it took to see what was under the costumes of the bartenders and waitresses when he and Max went to a gentleman's club. In most cases, they didn't strip on stage, or at all. But, most also had a price. Sometimes, Max and John would tell the waitresses that each time she brought them a drink, they would each put a couple dollars in the middle of the table and she had to decide at what point she would flash them, if at all. If she waited too long, and she didn't flash them before they decided it was the last round for them, they would take the money and the offer off the table. In all the time they have been doing that, it only failed them once. And, the most it ever cost them was thirty dollars.

"I just showed you my ass, sugar," she flirted. "What more do you want to see?"

"Well," he winked, "as I've stated, we're detectives."

Again, she smiled as she nodded.

"So, we are experts at deducing facts from fiction," he turned to Max. "Wouldn't you say that's about right, Detective Stone?" he said playfully.

Max cleared his throat as if he were about to say something official. "Uh, yes, you would be correct, Detective Thompson." He tried to sound police-like.

She winked at Max.

"Anyway," John continued, "the facts seem to be that we both, he and I" he said, motioning to his friend with his free hand, "like what we have seen and therefore, would like to investigate what is under your top."

Max was shaking his head, trying to disguise his smile. Angel too, was smiling as she pulled her hand away from his and playfully slapped Tank on his forearm.

"Why, detective," she faked a blush. "I'm an angel. I don't do that sort of thing." She giggled.

Max tipped up his glass and motioned to her that he would like another bourbon. John, seeing that he might fall behind, did the same. She turned to make their drinks, and when she turned back toward them, there was twenty dollars on the bar in the form of four five-dollar bills.

"Angel," John motioned to the money, "each time we order a drink, we're each putting five dollars in the middle until you decide we are worthy to have our eyes gaze upon the glory. He spent the next few minutes explaining their game.

By the third drink, they noticed their glasses arrived fuller than before: same price for the drink but more booze. This usually happened when you flirted with the bartender, and they knew that. It was all part of their game and a part of their plan. Most of the time, the men in these places didn't pay much attention to the bartenders because they didn't get to see them topless. Their attention, and their extra money, almost always went to the girls in G-strings, dancing on the poles.

The two sat there, sometimes with their backs to the bar and watched the dancers. Every three songs, the DJ would announce a new dancer to the center stage, as the girls were rotating among the three stages. Once in a while, a scantily clad woman would come by and flirt with them and ask if they were interested in a lap dance or a private dance in the V.I.P. lounge. She would quickly dismiss herself when she was turned down. The money between them had grown to forty dollars and still no sight of Angel's boobs.

Max noticed different ladies here and there as it was apparent the night shift was slowly filtering in. He looked at his watch and figured they had time for one more, and he and John ordered and each placed another five in the pot.

Angel placed their drinks in front of them.

"This is our last one, Angel," John flirted. "It looks like we'll have to take that money back." He smiled at her. "You know that will be the first time we ever had to do that."

"Such a pity, too," Max added, "I bet the view, well let's just say, is heavenly."

"Ok, ok," she giggled. "You two win." She lifted her top to reveal her firm, milky breasts. Nothing implanted here. They were absolutely perfect. Max particularly enjoyed the sight of her pierced left nipple. John stood and saluted as she quickly pulled her top back down.

She raked up her money. "Thank you, gentlemen. I hope it was worth it."

"Worth every penny," John quipped as he sat back down.

Max agreed.

"I would have done it for ten," she confessed with a big grin. "I just wanted to see how far you two would go."

The DJ announced that "Emerald" was taking the stage about the time Max swallowed the last of his Jim Beam. He looked toward the stage to check her out. Her back was to him as she danced. Her dark green spandex shorts barely concealed her apple-shaped bottom. Her bikini top, still on, matched her shorts. Her hair was reddish-blond and about shoulder length. She was twirling around the brass pole as the lights flashed.

Wait a minute, did he know her? No, it was highly doubtful. Perhaps he had arrested her at one time or another.

She twirled again and ripped off her top, exposing her breasts. He couldn't get a good look at her face. Still, there was something about her. He decided he needed a closer look.

Max slid off his barstool, dove into the sea of testosterone, and gradually made his way to the edge of the stage. Once again, she circled the brass pole. Finally, her emerald eyes met his. Only one person he knew in the entire world had eyes that color of green. Peggy Meece!

Chapter 30

Peggy's eyes exploded wide in surprise and embarrassment. She instantly covered herself with her hands and arms. Max ripped his coat from his body, jumped up on stage, threw it around her and began to escort her down the steps. Patrons began booing him for his interruption.

By the time they reached the bottom of the stairs, a large bouncer met them and caught Max by the arm. The bouncer pounced so quickly, it caught him off guard.

"Stop," she screamed at the bouncer, "I know him."

"I don't give a shit," the muscular man shouted. "Nobody touches the girls. Your ass is out of here, pal," he screamed at Max as he twisted his arm behind his back.

"You don't understand, I'm..."

"Shut the fuck up. I don't give a shit who you are."

Without warning, John's large arm found its mark and quickly encircled the neck of the bouncer. At the same time, he shoved the barrel of his pistol in the crack of the man's ass.

"Let him go now or I'm going to clean out your colon faster than a bottle of Golytely." John was gritty and stern.

The bouncer did as he was instructed.

Max turned and flashed his badge.

"Get the picture?" He barked at the large man.

The bouncer nodded as John holstered his pistol. Max looked around and noticed the scene had gathered a lot of attention. He flashed his badge again to the gathering crowd and demanded they all go about their business or risk arrest. They chose to go back to their drinks. The bouncer did likewise.

Peggy's head was in her hands. She was sobbing and embarrassed.

"I'm sorry, Peggy," Max said as he put his arm around her. "I don't understand what you are doing here."

She wiped away a tear. "No, Max, it is I who should be sorry."

She was very upset. Was it because he interrupted and interfered in her life? Was it embarrassment from having someone she knew on a professional level see her topless? Damn, she had been through so much lately.

So, this was the job she could go back to when she left the Coroner's office. No wonder she didn't want to talk about it.

John was still doing crowd control. Rumblings of the man with the gun were spreading. It wasn't the smartest thing Tank had ever done, but Max was happy he brought a quick end to the situation. Generally, you didn't really want people to know you were a cop and that you were packing heat, especially in a place like this.

"Max?" Peggy said. She gently caressed his cheek with the back of her hand.

She looked into his eyes and he noticed her mascara had run and created black lines down her cheeks. Damn her emerald green eyes were so mesmerizing, even when they were teary. One could easily get lost in those liquid pools.

"Yes, Peggy?"

"I don't belong here," she said quietly.

Max agreed.

"Will you take me home?" Her eyes filled with water again.

He was confused.

"I am so damned mixed up these days. I've always looked up to you and I so cherish your opinions," she said. "I just need a friend to talk to."

"Come on. I'll help you get home and we can talk a bit." He gave her a reassuring hug.

She excused herself to the dressing room to put on proper attire. Max talked with Tank and told him he would catch a cab with Peggy and then catch another cab after that to the precinct to get his car later. He understood.

"Be gentle, Stoney?" he said as he placed a hand on his shoulder. "Be gentle."

"You're such an ass." Max laughed as he swiped his arm away. "You know exactly what's going on."

"On a serious note, be careful. She's an emotional train wreck right now."

Max and Peggy rode mostly in silence, only occasionally engaging in idle chit-chat.

When they arrived at her apartment, she told Max to make himself comfortable. He tossed his coat on a chair and sat on the sofa as she excused herself.

Her apartment was neatly kept, well furnished, and brightly decorated. It was just as Max had pictured it would be, given her personality. He sat there in silence, rubbing the palms of his hands together for what seemed like five or ten minutes before she returned. She came from the bedroom wearing grey sweat pants and a baggy red IU sweatshirt. He caught a hint of her Eternity perfume as she passed him. He could pick that scent out anywhere. It was one of his favorites.

"Would you like something to drink or eat?" she asked as she switched on the kitchen light.

"Uh, sure," he replied as he stood and walked toward the kitchen. "What do you have?"

She opened the refrigerator. "Let me see." She placed a hand on her knee and leaned into the fridge.

"I have a diet soda, orange juice, some white wine, or I can make some coffee." She straightened. "Oh," she added, "and of course ice water."

Before Max could answer she asked if he was hungry, adding that she was in the mood for a snack. After a brief debate, she quickly prepared a plate of meat and cheese and invited Max to sit. She placed the plate on the table in front of him. She grabbed up some crackers, a bottle of white table wine and two wine glasses, sat down at the table across from him, and poured them each a glass. As she sat, Max noticed she folded her legs under her bottom. This amused him.

Over the next several minutes, they ate, laughed, and drank wine. He knew at some point the conversation would get serious and they would have to relive what had happened at the club. But, for now, she kept it light-hearted and that was fine with him. He figured she was trying to gather the courage to talk about what was on her mind.

She tipped her glass and drained her wine. She stood, scooped up the bottle, along with her empty glass, and invited Max to come and join her in the living room.

She put a Robin Thicke CD in the stereo and found a seat on the sofa next to Max, again folding her legs under her bottom. She filled both their glasses and sat the bottle on the coffee table.

"Max," she finally said. "I really appreciate you coming back here and allowing me to talk with you."

"No problem, Peggy, but we really haven't talked much about what's on your mind, except for wine, music, and food." He was cautious and sincere.

"I'm just so confused right now. I just..." She stopped as she choked back a tear.

"Well," he said as he turned toward her, "let's start with the stripping thing." He sipped from his glass. "I mean, how in the hell." He paused as he realized he was sounding more like a father than a friend. "I mean why?"

"I did it to make money when I was in college," she said shamefully. "I made good money, enough to pay for my college, in fact." She emptied her wine.

"You shouldn't be doing that."

"Yeah, yeah." She filled her glass. "I know, but I didn't want to spend another minute retrieving dead bodies."

She sipped again and looked at Max with admiration.

"How do you do it, Max?" she asked, "I mean, how do you live with all the death, blood, and destruction?"

"Well, it's not easy," he confessed, "I never really get used to it." He looked at her and smiled. "You know what they say, someone has to do it."

They spent the next several minutes talking about what was right and what was wrong with the world. She asked him how he came about being a detective and about his partner John. He told her the story about how his parents were killed during the middle of the night while he slept in the next room and how the murder had never been solved. He told her how he had vowed to do everything he could be avenge his parents murder.

She listened with a sad heart. She studied him as he spoke. She noticed his jaw clinch as the tension mounted in his voice. She watched him with new admiration. He was a soulful man, soft and gentle. She had certainly never seen this side of him. She liked it. She wondered how often he showed it. Most every time she ever saw him was during an investigation or a crime scene and he was always on edge and professional. Oh, he had a humorous side. She liked that about him. She had seen it from time to time. He was chiseled, stern, and quite sexy. To her, he was a sexy older man, the kind of man any woman would want. She always thought so, but she was only in her mid-twenties. He was the kind of guy a person could look up to and admire; the kind of guy you could seek advice from and the kind of guy you could confide in. She felt safe around him, like nothing could hurt her. She watched his face intently as he told about how he found his parents dead the next morning. She noticed a tear well up in his lake blue eyes, which were dimming to a gray color.

"Max," she said quietly as she slid closer and touched his face. "I'm sorry that happened to you." She gently brushed the tear from his eye.

"Uh, thanks," he managed. "I shouldn't have told you those things." He apologized.

"No," she reassured him, "I'm glad you did. I see you in a whole new light. I understand more about what makes you who you are." She smiled as she looked in his eyes.

There were those damn emerald green eyes again, staring him right in the face. What was it about a woman's eyes? He had always been told a woman's eyes were the window to their souls. At that moment, truer words were never spoken.

He looked at her face, bright with her makeup. Her freckles under her eyes were light and gave her that baby-doll look. She pulled his face with her hand and kissed him on the cheek.

"Thank you for helping me with my problem. I feel much better about that situation now. I don't know what I'm going to do but I now realize that stripping isn't the answer." She smiled as she allowed him to sit upright again.

"Well, you're very welcome, Peggy." He patted her on the leg, trying to regain his composure.

"And thank you for sharing a piece of your soul with me," she said softly.

Max did not get the words thank you out as Peggy jumped on his lap, grabbed him around the neck, and pressed her lips to his. Her lips were full and warm, and she smelled terrific. Even under her baggy sweatshirt, Max could feel her breasts press against him.

He felt his passion swell. He desired her and he wanted her. He liked what he had seen at the strip club and wandered what she would feel like if he touched her. He wanted nothing more than to throw her on the floor and devour her, but should he? After all, he was married.

Chapter 31

For a moment, Max allowed the invasion, but then realized, what was happening. And, what was about to happen was wrong on more than one level.

He gently pushed her back. She was breathing hard.

"Peggy? What are you doing?"

She stood. "I'm sorry, Max. I don't know what came over me." She jumped up and ran crying to the bedroom.

"Peggy? Wait."

He followed her and stood in the doorway, refusing to go into the bedroom. She was lying across her bed.

"Peggy?" he said gently. "You ok?"

She turned to face him. "I'm very sorry, Max. I don't know what got into me. I wanted to thank you for all your help and that was the only way I knew how," she confessed.

"That's just silly, but don't sweat it. First of all, you don't need to thank me. That's what friends are for.

199

Second, you should never lower yourself to trading sex for favors."

She got up from the bed and approached him, hesitating when she was in front of him.

"I must admit, I think you are very sexy. I have always thought that. And, I am attracted to you. I wasn't just looking to trade sex for favors. I would do anything to have you. Sometimes, I think my thoughts about you run deeper than merely a crush."

Max was stunned. He didn't know how to respond to that.

"Uh, thank you," he finally said.

"Is it ok to hug you?" She forced slight smile.

He held out his arms. "Of course it is."

"You hate me?" she asked as she slid her arms around him.

He was amused. "Of course not. I'm actually flattered," he confessed. "It's not every day a beautiful woman throws herself at me."

The two returned to the sofa, finished off the bottle of wine, and talked some more.

"I've always wanted to ask you, Peggy, how did you wind up at the Coroner's office? That line of work does not suit you at all."

"Well, Max, It's a long story. Basically, my father and my grandfather were Coroners and I felt like I wanted to follow in their footsteps. Pretty dumb huh?"

"No, not at all. I mean, I chose police work sort of because of my parents. But, other than that, what was the attraction to the work. You had to know what you were getting in to. I mean, you had to know it wasn't glamorous and it dealt with dead bodies."

"It's not the dead bodies, per se, that gets me. There were a lot of times it didn't bother me much. But, when they assigned me to retrieving murdered and mutilated bodies..., that really got to me; especially the ones with the girls more my age.

"Yeah, that even pulls at my old heart."

They sat in silence for a moment, reflecting. She offered to open another bottle of wine but Max thought they shouldn't.

He watched her as she kept tracing her index finger around the rim of her empty glass. She was uncomfortable with the subject of death and murder. Max knew that. He had admiration for her. It wasn't easy to bare your feelings the way she did. His heart went out to her. She was so confused with life right now. It didn't seem fair. Her whole life was ahead of her and she didn't need to be spending it around evil-doers and the destruction they left behind.

"How long had you been working at the Coroner's office?" Max broke the silence.

"Not long. Only about three months before I met you and John so, about six months in total."

"That's not too long, which is good."

"What do you mean?"

"Well, after a while, the stuff gets so ingrained in your memory and daily life that it's hard to shed. But you shouldn't have too much trouble. So, that's good." He smiled.

"I hope so. I've had a few nightmares since seeing those girls tied down and cut up like that. It brought back memories of my friend, Shannon, from high school."

"What happened?"

"She was abducted by a man during her junior year and they found her dead body two months later in a field." Her eyes filled with tears. "She had been tortured."

He reached over and placed a hand on her leg. "I'm so sorry, Peggy."

She used the sleeve of her hoodie and wiped her eyes. "It's ok. I think about it sometimes."

He hadn't counted on that. It was no wonder she got so emotional. Hell that would be enough to shove anyone over the edge.

"So," Max said, trying to change the subject. "Peggy, what are you going to do now? You shouldn't be stripping and I don't think going back to the Coroner's office is a good option either."

"I don't know." She shrugged her shoulders.

"What are you interested in?"

"Well," she thought for a moment. "I've always been fascinated in police work." She smiled at him.

"Be serious."

"I am. Since meeting you, I've always thought what you do is awesome."

"Well, you don't just become a detective. You usually start as a beat cop and it takes years of hard word, dedication, and study."

"I know that," she giggled. "But I still think what you do is amazing. You're amazing."

"So, what else you like?"

"Some of the classes I took included evidence gathering and forensic work."

"Really? That might be a good fit for you." Max contemplated the thought. "You know, I wonder if Terry Green can use anyone in the forensics lab."

"Seriously?" She grew excited. "Would you talk to him for me?"

"Sure, why not? I'll talk to Terry and see if I can pull any strings for you."

She thanked him over and over.

Max looked at his watch. It read 11:43 p.m. and decided he better go home so he called for a cab. He had a long day of work ahead of him tomorrow. She walked him to the door. He told her to call him if she needed him.

She thanked him again and threw her arms around his neck to hug him. God she felt good and she smelled delicious. Her breasts were, once again, pressed against him. Max rolled his eyes upward as if to say to God, *"God, I know you're testing me and you need to know that I was just a C student."*

A few minutes after Max had left, his cell phone rang. He assumed it was Leah checking on him.

"Greetings, Mr. Stone," the sandpapered voice said.

"So, it's you again." Max angered instantly. "When you going to quit playing games and face me man to man?" Max gritted his teeth.

"In time, Mr. Stone."

His voice was its usual slow and deliberate monotone. It was deep and rough. His voice sounded like he gargled with bourbon and dirt.

"I can't wait to get my hands on you and you know I'm going to do it."

"And I can't wait to get my hands on your precious Leah." the mysterious person mocked.

"Meet me right now, damn you!" Max commanded. "I'll kill you right now!"

"Temper, temper, Mr. Stone," he said calmly. "I merely wanted to ask you a couple of questions."

Max sat in silence.

"Mr. Stone," the voice said. "Do you think it wise you leave Leah alone like that?"

"What do you mean?"

"Well, I've been watching her and I've been watching you."

Max was speechless. A moment later, the voice broke the silence.

"Do you think Leah would approve of the little dish you were with tonight?" he taunted.

Shit, he had been watching Max, and that pissed him off. "How was the little red headed girl? I bet she was amazing and scrumptious."

Max was seething. His pulse pounded in his temples. "You don't know what the hell you're talking about."

"Don't I? Unless you are terrible at closing the deal, Detective Stone, Emerald should have been a sure thing. I mean, after all, how hard is it to score with a stripper?"

The prick had been at the strip club, watching him.

"I wonder if Leah would approve." He mocked.

The phone went silent and he was gone.

At that moment, a terrible thought crossed Max's mind. Up until now, he had thought Peggy was a sweet, confused young woman. Did she only make a confession tonight about her feelings or did she also confess something else without knowing it? Was getting him to her apartment, hell, everything surrounding her, a ruse? She said she would do anything to have him. Did that include murder? Did she actually commit, or know anything about, the murders of those young girls? Was it all a plan to get Leah out of the picture? No, it can't be. The phone calls he's been getting were male voices. Could she have an accomplice? That was stretching things, wasn't it? Hell, his head was spinning.

Chapter 32

Max crawled into bed. Leah didn't budge. He let his thoughts of the phone call drift him off to sleep. He barely remembered his head hitting the pillow.

The alarm woke him way too early. His batteries weren't yet charged.

"Well, how did your, uh, investigation go last night," she said, rubbing sleep from her eyes.

"It went well," he smiled feeling guilt. "I'm running late this morning. I have a big day. Do you have that list I asked for?"

"Yeah, it's in an envelope on the kitchen counter."

He kissed her and turned to leave.

"Honey?" She called to him.

"Yes?" He turned to face her.

"What do you need that list for anyway?"

"It's part of the investigation of Misty Lawrence and," he hesitated to tell her his hunch but decided against it, "well, the investigation." He left it at that and grabbed up the list.

"That list is rather confidential. Please try your best to keep it that way, ok?" She slid out of bed.

"Sure, baby. I understand."

Tank was already at his desk waiting for him. On any given day, Max would be the first to work, but today, Tank was waiting for details with his encounter with Peggy Meece.

"Did you introduce her to ol' Stoney?" he teased.

"I could have," Max simply stated. He saw no reason to go into any details of his evening or his thoughts.

"Are you serious?" Tank was curious as he leaned on his desk. "Tell me you're not serious."

"Oh, but I am, my friend," Max assured.

"And," Tank drew out slowly. He gestured with his hand, seeking details.

"I didn't."

"Wow, how in the hell could you turn that down? I mean, I know you're married and all of that, but," his thoughts drifted. "Damn, it might have been worth the risk."

"Would you get serious, Tank."

John shook a finger at his best friend. "You're a good man, Max Stone," he chuckled. "Hell, when Leah gets tired of your sorry ass, I may just have to grab you up for myself."

Max told Tank what had actually happened at Peggy Meece's apartment and how his heart went out to her. She did, in fact, make a pass at him. Perhaps it was the wine or perhaps it was his soft side, hell he didn't know. It could have been just her getting caught up in the moment. Maybe she thought that was how she was supposed to act when she had a man over. On any other moment on any other day, and, if he were single, he would love to be with someone like Peggy. She was beautiful from the top down and had a warm soul, or so it seemed. For all he knew it was part of a plan to eliminate Leah. In any event, she was sensual and she was young.

"I must still have it," Max proclaimed.

"Well, you know, I'd date you." Tank joked as he made kissing sounds at him.

"That's so comforting."

Max unfolded the list from his pocket.

"What's that?"

"It's the list of people that attended Leah's seminar a couple of weeks ago."

"Oh, yeah," Tank said. "Let's have a look."

They scanned the list of names, mostly girls, with the exception of seven boys. Max expected to find the name Misty Lawrence, which he did. A few names below, he found the name Kaliani Sun. The two looked at one-another simultaneously.

The blood drained from Max's face. "Well, I'm starting to see a pattern, and that disturbs me."

"No shit. What is there, like seventeen or eighteen names of girls on this list? Does someone intend to kill all these girls? And, where the hell do we start?"

"I think we go back to the college and see Dean Propst. We need to get the word to everyone on this list, and fast."

Tank agreed.

Max's cell phone rang. It was Terry Green from forensics.

"Hello, Terry," Max said.

"Max, I hate to ruin your day but you need to get over here right away." His voice was somber.

"Slow down, Terry. Over where and what's up?"

"I'm at the Fort Harrison Park." He paused and took a deep breath. "Max, we've found another girl."

Max hung up the phone. Tank could see the distance in his eyes and knew that it was not good news. Max's thoughts turned to Peggy Meece. Oh God! Please don't let it be Peggy Meece. He didn't want it to be anybody, but please not Peggy Meece. The killer had been watching him and he knew where Peggy lived. He knew everything he needed to make her his next prey. And, if it was Peggy, how did she equate to all of this?

"Max?" John broke his thoughts. "What's going on?"

"We'll have to look deeper into this list later. We've got to go. They found another girl."

Chapter 33

The two detectives arrived at Fort Harrison Park. The park was a decommissioned military base honoring President Benjamin Harrison. It was located on the northeast side of the city.

They went through the entrance and made their way to the location they had been given. Flashing lights and crime scene tape told them they were in the right place.

They were immediately greeted by Terry Green.

"She's down this way, guys," he said after shaking their hands.

They followed him to the start of a trail, which led down into the woods toward Fall Creek.

She was anchored to the ground near the water.

"The sick bastard isn't prejudice," Max said as he looked down at the girl.

"Max, is that very appropriate?" John said.

"No, that's not what I mean," Max explained. "He has killed a Caucasian girl, an Asian girl, and now this girl. So, what I mean is there is no pattern."

She was a black girl, with beautiful ebony skin. She was young, collage age, and very petite. Her hair was jet black, straight. Her make-up was unblemished, except for the tear stains down her cheeks, and her lipstick was bright red and not smudged. Like the others, she was naked, except for her royal blue bra that covered her small breasts, and blood had caked around the incisions that ran the length of both sides of her abdomen.

"Note?" Max asked Terry.

"Yep, just like the others, proclaiming to need her reproduction organs."

"Do we know her name or anything?"

"Yes," Terry handed Max a slip of paper. "Her name is Anastasia Stylez. She is a student at IUPUI, according to her Jag Tag."

"Jag Tag?" John asked.

"Her student I.D."

"Who found her?" Max asked.

"A deer hunter."

"Bullshit," Max spat. "Where is he? Did you question him at length?"

"Of course, why?" Terry questioned.

"They don't allow deer hunting in this park." Max's tone was forceful.

"Well, that's what we thought. So, we thought, perhaps, the killer screwed up," Terry said. "But, when we checked with the DNR, we found they are, in fact, having an organized deer hunt today and tomorrow only in order to cut down on the deer population." Terry paused. "He even had the special permit on him from the DNR, so his story checked out."

Max was angry. "You know, it's almost like this guy wants us to know he's targeting college girls by leaving the student I.D. on them. The damn water is right there," Max pointed. "He could just have easily thrown the I.D. in the water, or took it with him all together."

"And I'll tell you something else," John added, "he's smart. He wants us to find the bodies."

"What do you mean, John?" Terry asked.

John spent the next few minutes explaining his theory. Misty Lawrence had been found in Eagle Creek near the water. She was beside a very popular trail for bird watching and jogging, even in the winter. Kaliana Sun was found at Broad Ripple Park, also near the water, but just off a popular jogging trail. Now, Anastasia Stylez was found way off the beaten path at Ben Harrison Park, but during an organized deer hunt. The killer had to know all three girls would be found quickly.

"That makes a lot of sense, Tank," Max said, patting his partners shoulder. "Good work."

"Yes, perfect sense," Terry added.

The three continued discussing as forensics were sweeping the area for any clues.

"Any possible leads, Max?" Terry asked.

"No." Max was deep in thought. "But I think I might know where to get one." He motioned for Tank to follow.

"Where?" Terry yelled out behind them.

"My wife," Max shouted back over his shoulder.

Terry was perplexed. "Do what?"

Chapter 34

"Leah?" Tank questioned. "Stoney, you know I always trust your judgment, but I'm beginning to think you're losing it. How the hell is she going to give you a lead?"

"That list," Max said as they reached the car.

He dug out the list, unfolded it, and let his eyes scan the page.

"Shit!" he exclaimed.

"What is it?"

"Look at this," Max said, shoving the paper under John's nose.

There it was in black and white. Anastasia Styles name appeared, along with the first two victims. Unfortunately, there were many other names too. How could one make a pattern from this? The names of seven guys were on the list as well. Suspects? Perhaps. Future victims? Not Likely. So far, only girls had been killed. But why? And how far did the killer intend to go?

Max retrieved his cell phone and dialed Leah.

"Hi baby!" she said cheerfully.

"Hey, sweetie," he replied.

She could tell by the tone that he was stressed and had a lot on his mind.

"What's up, babe," she said with a more controlled tone.

"That list you gave me?"

"Yes?"

He didn't really know where to begin. He couldn't tell her too much, but he needed to ask her just enough to get the answers he needed. He hadn't thought it through and wasn't exactly sure what to ask and how to ask it.

"What is it, honey?" she asked again.

"You remember telling me that Misty Lawrence was at your seminar?"

"Yes?"

"Well, I expected to find her name on the list you gave me," he stumbled out.

"Well, of course," she said with concern. "What is it?"

"Didn't you tell me she approached you about donating eggs or something?" he managed.

"Yes, honey. What's going on?"

"Does the name Kaliani Sun ring a bell?" he asked. "Her name is on your list too."

215

"Yes! She was one of the girls, along with Misty, that approached me after the seminar about donating eggs. Why?"

Max was definitely starting to see a pattern now, perhaps a motive; egg donation. Well, at least a link. He had to proceed with caution.

"How many girls, in total, came and talked to you?"

"Let me see," she thought for a moment. "I believe there were a total of four. Why?" she asked again with a little more force.

"What four?" he demanded.

"Well, Misty, of course, and Kaliani too," she stopped to think.

"Who else, who else!" he shouted. He realized he was getting too forward and changed his attitude. "Honey," he started over, "this is important. Do you remember the names of the other two girls?"

She racked her brain, but the names were escaping her memory.

"I don't remember, honey, but I do remember one of them was an African-American," she said as she desperately tried to remember the names.

Well, the black girl was obviously Anastasia Stylez, but that didn't really help too much. He already knew her name was on the list. There were likely a number of African-American women on the list besides Anastasia Stylez. What he needed was a way to narrow the list down. Was everyone on that list in danger? That thought scarred the hell out of him.

Max was beginning to formulate motives and possibilities in his mind. The killer could be someone who attended the class. Any of them could have competition issues, perhaps jealously. If they eliminated a few then their own grades and future could look better, and more prosperous, providing they could pull it off. This was not a likely scenario in his mind, but it was something.

On the other hand, since the three victims were women who had sought to further the research by giving eggs, a more likely candidate would be someone who was against Stem Cell research. Likely, yes, but who?

"Max," Leah said, dissolving his thoughts. "I just thought of something."

"Yes?" he replied eagerly, "what is it?"

"I remember the black girl had a name like, Fantasia or something like that, and the other girl's last name was like a car, I think," she said.

Of course Fantasia was actually Anastasia. That confirmed that all three victims had talked to Leah about donating eggs. Was the fourth girl going to be a fourth victim? Max scanned the paper again. There! There was the name of Melody Ford; last name like a car. It was the only name like that. It had to be Melody Ford.

"Could the name of the other girl be Melody Ford?" he asked her.

She thought for a moment. "Yes! Yes, that's it!" she exclaimed. "Max, why?"

"I've got to go," he said. "Call you later."

Max hung up the phone and repeated everything to his partner.

"We've got to find this Melody Ford, and damn quick."

"Stoney," John said. "I don't want to alarm you, but this girl's death is closer to your house than the previous two."

Chapter 35

They fired up the car and made tracks toward the campus. Max's next call was to the Dean of the school, Craig Propst. It was mid-afternoon so Max hoped he could catch him there. He figured it would be the perfect and quickest way to get vital information on a student. Surely, the school would have current contact information and an address on Melody Ford.

"Dean Propst," Max spoke when he answered his phone, "this is Detective Max Stone. I need a favor and I need it now" "Certainly, Detective Stone. Anything at all."

"I need to know where I can find one of your students. Her name is Melody Ford," he paused. "Dr. Propst, I believe she may be in great danger!"

"Right away, Detective," he promised.

Max heard him lay the receiver down with a clunk on his desk and bark out orders to his assistant. It seemed like it took an hour for him to return to the phone.

"Detective?" he spoke, "her records show she lives at the Canal Apartments on West Street. They are right across from the campus."

"Apartment number?" Max asked.

"Um, 406," he replied.

Max mashed the pedal and his car responded as they worked their way through light traffic to the other side of town. Luckily, it was early afternoon.

It took Max only fifteen minutes to navigate his way across the city. The trip normally took thirty. He pulled the car to a screeching halt in front of the Canal Apartments. Dean Propst was standing outside.

"Detective," he hurried up to Max as he jumped out of the car, "I took it upon myself to call the number given in her file and got no answer so I rushed over."

"No answer on her door either?" Max asked.

"I don't know. I just got here," he said.

Max spoke as they walked. "Is the number you called her home number or her cell?"

"I don't know, but it's the only number we have on record," he said. "I do know that most students only have a cell phone."

They found apartment 406 and Max banged on the door. No answer. He banged again, and began drawing a crowd from other apartments, wondering what all the banging was. John, flashed his badge to the grumbling people, doing his usual crowd control and telling people to go back to whatever they were doing. After the third knock, Max gave up and sent Tank down to the manager's office to retrieve a master key. Moments later, he returned with the manager.

"I'm sorry, sir, but I cannot let you go in there without permission," the aging, frail man said.

"Break the door down, Tank," Max commanded his large partner.

"Right," He brushed past the manager.

"Wait!" he demanded. "You can't just do that without a warrant, officer," his excited voiced squeaked.

"Look," Max said in an agitated state, "either you open the door for us or we will do it ourselves. The woman who lives here may be in danger. Did my partner not explain that to you and did he not show you his badge?"

"Well, yes he did, but..."

"This door is going to get opened and opened now," Max interrupted. "How it gets opened is up to you."

The manager stood frozen in place. Was he contemplating whether or not to open the door? Was he showing a sign of defiance? Hell, either way it was taking too long and Max had already lost his patience. He nodded at Tank and with one quick motion his foot came up and slammed into the door, blasting it wide open.

The manager's eyes went wide and he could not believe what he had just witnessed.

Raven, Max's trusty pistol had snapped into his hand and was at the ready as they entered the apartment.

"You stay outside," John commanded to the Dean and to the manager.

The two detectives crept in and shouted "police." No answer. Beer had been spilled on the counter and the can holding it had rolled a few feet from it and lay empty on its side. It was apparent that no attempt had been made to clean it up. Several other beer cans, most empty, had been strewn around the kitchenette area and counter.

From the living room, the television was on. John yelled again, but there was no response. They turned the corner, saw the T.V. but there was nobody watching the program that was on. On the coffee table were many more empty beer cans.

On the kitchen table was some unopened mail, nothing unusual here. The bathroom, too, checked out ok. Then they opened the door to her bedroom. Everything seemed to be in its place except for one thing. There was no Melody Ford.

Chapter 36

"Dean Propst, you know it is basically, mid-morning. Shouldn't Melody be in class right now?" Max asked.

"Normally, yes. I checked that out before I met you here. She is supposed to be in class but, according to her professor, she didn't show up for class today. She hasn't been to any of her classes."

Max feared he was too late. His heart sank. He figured sometime today he was going to get a call that they had yet another girl and he was certain it was going to be Melody Ford.

"However," the Dean continued. "I checked her attendance records and, although Ms. Ford is a wonderful student, academically, she does lack in attendance. And," he continued. "She has a bit of a reputation of being a partier."

Suddenly, the door to the apartment across the hall opened. A young man, maybe twenty, appeared.

"Are you gentlemen looking for Melody?"

"Yes, do you know where she is?" Max asked as he flashed his badge.

"I don't know where she is but I saw her being led out of here late last night by, I think, her boyfriend. It looked like she was really drunk or drugged or something."

"Do you know the name of the person she left with?"

"Yes, his name is Brad, um," he paused to think. "His name is Brad Mitchell.

Max quickly whipped out the list he had tucked in his pocket. The name Brad Mitchell was, in fact, among the seven men on the list.

"Was he inebriated too?"

"He didn't appear to be."

"Can you give me a description of him?"

For the next few minutes, Max jotted down the basic description of Brad Mitchell. He also wrote down additional details that outlined what he and Melody Ford were wearing when they were last seen.

"Do you know what he drives?"

"Yeah, he drives a red Camaro."

"Do you know the approximate year of the vehicle?"

"I'm sorry. I don't."

"Do you know where they might have gone?"

"No sir, I'm afraid I don't."

Max turned to John. "Go down and call headquarters. Have them put out a bulletin to stop and check every red Camaro they see."

"Sure thing."

He turned to the Dean. "Dean, can you call your office to confirm if this, Brad Mitchell, is a student at your college and, if so, get me any information on him you can."

"Sure thing." He produced his cell and immediately dialed his office.

John returned from the car and informed Max the bulletin had gone out. Max then turned to the young man from across the hall, got additional information from him, along with contact information, and allowed him to go about his business.

"Uh, Detective?"

"Yes, Dean?"

"Brad Mitchell is a student," he said while scribbling an address on a piece of paper. "Here is his address."

Max grabbed the paper. "Thanks. My partner and I will be in touch."

They shook hands with the Dean, dismissed themselves, jumped into the car, and headed for Brad Mitchel's.

Chapter 37

The red Camaro they were seeking was absent from the driveway of the small suburban home.

Max rapped on the door and was greeted by middle-aged woman.

"Hello, ma'am, I'm detective, Max Stone," he said as he showed her his badge.

She was hesitant but returned the greeting. She introduced herself as Barbara Mitchell.

"We are looking for Bradley Mitchell. Do you know his whereabouts?"

"What do you want with my son? What did he do?"

"Mrs. Mitchell," Max cautioned.

"It's Miss," she corrected him.

"We're not sure he did anything at this point." Max decided he better play it cool. "We are actually looking for Melody Ford."

"That harlot? What's the bitch gone and done now?" She interrupted again.

It was clear she did not approve of her son being involved with Melody. Max wondered why that was.

"Miss Mitchell, this is extremely important. We fear Melody Ford may be in grave danger and it is imperative we find her quickly."

"And you think my son..."

She was hostile and stand-offish. He wondered if it ran in the family. He needed all the information he could obtain from her so he decided he better keep the conversation lite.

"No, no, we are not suggesting that, ma'am. Melody was last seen with your son so we are trying to locate him so we can, hopefully, find her. In fact, if they are together and she is in danger, it may put him in danger as well."

He hoped the logic would reward him with information.

Her stance weakened. "I haven't seen him since last night. After dinner, he left and went to her place."

"Is that normal behavior for him?"

"It has been since he started going with that whore."

"We've been to her place, ma'am. They weren't there. Do you know where we might locate them? Is there a place they like to hang out that you can think of?"

She thought for a moment. "Nope. He spends most of his nights and evenings with her. I would have assumed you would find them naked in her bed."

"Thank you for your time, Miss Mitchell. If you should hear from him, please give me a call," Max said as he handed her his card.

"Well, what am I supposed to do, detective? The boy's twenty-one now. Nothing I can do about it, I suppose," she said as if she were trying to avoid judgment. "He's just like his father. He likes women. His father left me for another woman and he leaves me alone for a woman too."

"Thank you, ma'am," Max said again.

Chapter 38

Another twenty-four hours had passed and nothing new had developed in the case. Max had fully expected to get a call informing him they had found the girl's dead body but, happily, he had not received any such call. Of course, that could be because they just hadn't located her body yet, but he had to hold out hope.

So far, thirty-seven red, or similar colored, Camaros had been stopped and searched by law enforcement; none containing Bradley Mitchell or Melody Ford.

Surveillance of her apartment and of his home produced similar results.

Max's cell rang. It was Terry Green.

"Max, we've located the red Camaro."

"Great. What about Bradley Mitchell."

"Max, he's dead."

"Dead? What do you mean he's dead?"

"I mean someone shot him in the head.

"And Melody Ford?"

"Not in the car with him. You better get over here."

Max wrote down the location and he and John immediately went to the railroad yard on the city's south side.

The victim was slumped in the driver's seat. It was clear a high-caliber round had been fired into his cranium from point-blank range. Half of his head had been blown off and pieces of bone fragment and brain matter were splattered in the back seat.

"Something about this doesn't add up." Max said to John.

"What do you mean?"

"I'm wondering if this is related to the killing of those girls or if it's something all-together different."

John wanted him to elaborate.

"Up until now, only women have been targeted, right?"

"Right," John agreed.

"Now, to go a step further, up until now, only girls that have donated eggs for research have been targeted. Although Bradley Mitchell's name does appear on the list, how does it fit? He can't donate eggs."

"True. So, do you think everyone on the list is in danger?"

"It's hard to say, but it looks that way. We need to find Melody Ford. It appears she is the only remaining survivor or the egg donators."

"Do you think she killed him? Hell, killed all of them?"

"I don't know."

They stood in silence for a moment.

"Max," John said. "A thought just crossed my mind."

"I'm open to suggestions."

"Perhaps Melody killed those girls out of jealously or something like that. The eyewitness told us she was very drunk."

"Yeah."

"So, do you think, during her drunken stupor, she spilled the beans to her boyfriend so she killed him to keep him quiet?"

"It's possible, but something still doesn't feel right about it."

"What do you mean?"

"Ok, let's assume, for a moment, she is the killer."

"I'm listening."

"If true, she sliced the abdomens of the other girls and stole their reproductive organs, right?"

John agreed.

"Well, most killers, especially serial killers, operate in a similar fashion. It doesn't make sense."

"That's true. However, she couldn't kill her boyfriend the same way, now could she? He doesn't exactly have the same reproductive organs."

"I know that, dumbass," Max said. "I mean if she did kill the other three, than how does he fit into the equation?"

"Again, I say it was out of necessity."

"Possible," Max agreed. "On the other hand, we've also been operating on the theory it could be someone against stem-cell research. She is in the program and obviously for the research."

"I say jealously."

"Possible, I guess. I've heard of stranger things. There's just one more thing bothering me."

"What's that?"

"Those calls I've been getting."

"What about them?" John asked.

"I know they are connected to all of this and I know it's the killer. The voice always seems to be a man."

John knew where he was going with it. "The voice could be disguised."

"I thought about that but it would have to be an amazing disguise. Also, if Melody Ford is the killer, why would she want to kill Leah?"

"Again, I think it's all about jealousy."

"It could be, I suppose," Max said. "In any event, let's go talk with Dean Propst and have him round up everyone on that list. All of them need to be warned and advised to keep careful watch of their surroundings."

John agreed.

They talked more about their theories and possibilities as they sped toward the college. They were still unsure if they were any closer to solving the crime. What they did know was that they had three dead girls, who had donated eggs for research, and a fourth girl missing. They now had a dead man, until now, was a possible suspect. He, too, had attended the seminar. And, somehow, all of this tied directly to Leah Stone.

"Hey Max?" John said.

"Yeah?"

"Is it possible that Melody Ford killed Bradley Mitchell out of self-defense? I mean, if he was the killer and was attempting to kill her, could she have killed him to save herself?"

"I thought of that, but, if that were true, where is she?"

"That's the million dollar question."

Chapter 39

The next morning, Leah arrived at work and things were pretty much normal. Freda Lyle was chipper while Doug Brewer, on the other hand, was his usual pompous self. Most of the morning was uneventful and it was business as usual. Leah and Freda cut up with one another. Doug scoffed at their behavior.

Most of the time, he let them be, deciding not to engage in their topics of conversation. Only occasionally, did they talk about something that mattered to him and he would inevitably put in his two cents worth. This morning, he overheard them talking about Max going to a strip club.

"I can't believe you would allow your, um, man to be so distasteful," he injected in their conversation with gall.

Leah turned from her conversation with Freda to address his remark. "And what business is it of yours?"

He sneered at her. "I am merely saying, Miss Stone," he paused. "He is a married man, is he not?" He continued without a response. "Married men should not be lusting after half-naked women at strip clubs."

"And why would that matter to you?"

"And you," he lowered his glasses to make his point. "Shame on you for allowing it. It's immoral."

Freda chuckled under her breath. This sort of debating happened quite often between Leah and Doug. He was always on a power trip and she was, well, she was just feisty. She knew how to push his buttons and had fun with it when he decided to be an ass.

"So, you disapprove of me letting my husband go to a strip club?" she asked.

"Indeed, I do."

"What if it's in the name of an investigation?" You do know he is a detective, don't you?"

"Yes, Miss Stone," he replied. "I do know his chosen line of work, although why I don't know. But do you mean to stand there before me and God and try to make me believe he didn't look at women?"

"I'm sure Max did, but that doesn't matter to me." She turned to Freda and smiled. "He is all man you know."

Doug turned in a huff and went about his business. If the truth were told, he probably had no opinion either way, but he loved to debate her and get her blood boiling.

The strip club and the mention of Max's current investigation brought up the discussion of the recent murders of two young college girls. These murders had been dominating the headlines for the past two weeks. Only Misty Lawrence's name had been mentioned, so far, in the paper. Leah remembered her from her seminar. She was a sweet, bright girl with a huge future in front of her. The only thing known about the second girl was that she was killed in the same fashion.

"Ladies, must we talk about such horrible things?"

"Does the subject bother you?" Freda asked him sincerely.

"Well," he paused, "as a matter of fact, it does."

Silence struck the room. Leah and Freda looked at one another with surprise in his statement. He always seemed cold and uncaring about most everything.

A few moments passed, he turned back toward them and broke the silence.

"Don't you find it disturbing that someone has killed off two bright young souls?"

"Well, yes, I do," Leah replied, "but..."

"As, do I," he interrupted, "so I would appreciate a change in conversation.

Appreciate? He actually used the word appreciate? Leah and Freda were speechless. Did they actually find something that bothered Doug Brewer? They had always thought his heart was black coal. Now, it appeared, he really did have a heart, if only a small one.

"Oh, Miss Stone," he said. "I find myself in need of a ride to pick up my car today. I had to take it in for repairs. Would you oblige?" he said sincerely.

Never in a million years would she ever think about doing any sort of favor for this jerk. For some reason, today, she felt a little less hostile toward him. Perhaps it was the revelation that something as tragic as young girls being murdered could actually bother him. To Leah, his personality had gone from ice cold to, well let's just say, chilly. Hell, even that was an improvement. Besides, he was a co-worker and, whether he liked it or not, she was his boss.

"Sure, Doug," she said with a smile, "after work ok?"

"Actually, could we leave a little early?" he asked. "I told the repair shop I would be there around 4:30."

"Sure, no problem." She shuddered at the thought of spending time with him outside of work.

Chapter 40

Max racked his brain. It had been nearly thirty-six hours since Melody Ford had been seen or heard from and the only person who may know her whereabouts, Bradley Mitchell, was dead.

He kept himself busy, spending his morning in and out of meetings. He and John spent time in Captain Lee's office discussing the case and he met with Terry Green to see if anything had developed on the forensic side.

While meeting with Terry, he took the opportunity to talk with him about Peggy Meece and the possibility of her working with him in the forensic lab. Terry agreed to interview her and told Max to have her call him.

Max grabbed a cup of coffee, and returned to his desk. He phoned Peggy and gave her the news. She was ecstatic.

He browsed the paper, reading the story of the dead man found in his car and his thoughts returned to the investigation. He spent most of last night lying awake in bed, playing everything in his mind. Something wasn't adding up, but he couldn't place his finger on it. He felt like the answer was right there but the solution was so far away. What was he missing? It tormented him.

He played the killer's phone calls over and over in his head. During the first call, the killer told him he would prove to the world the he wasn't a good cop and that he couldn't protect his family. The killer was only trying to get into his psyche. It was beginning to work. For the first time, doubt was creeping in.

Max's cell rang. As if on cue, the stranger was on the line.

"Hello, Mr. Stone," the recondite voice said. "It's a pity about the boy, don't you think?"

Anger leapt into Max's eyes. "I'm gonna get you, you son-of-a-bitch," he screamed as his face turned crimson.

"Now, now, Mr. Stone, is that any way to talk to someone who is trying to help you?"

Max decided to dig for information. "Tell me something."

"And what would you like to know, Mr. Stone? How I intend to kill Leah?"

He ignored the comment. "You say you killed the boy?"

"Indeed."

"Up until then, you only killed girls. More specifically, you only killed girls that donated eggs for research."

"Yes," the stranger interrupted.

"So, why Brad Mitchell? I mean, it's obvious you know the list of attendees to my wife's seminar at the school. How, I don't know, but I will figure it out. There are a total of twenty-four names on that list, including his. Do you intend to kill the remaining twenty?" Max was near-screaming and he was gathering an audience around his desk.

"Isn't this delicious," the stranger said with glee at his torment of Max. "No, unfortunately for Mr. Mitchell, Mr. Stone, he was in the wrong place at the wrong time. He was standing between me and Miss Ford so he had to be eliminated." His voice was deep and slow.

"So, your intentions are to only kill the girls that donated eggs? Why?"

Max's throat grew dry. He gulped the remainder of his coffee.

"Now, Mr. Stone, as I have said, I intend to prove you pale as a detective. I will not tell you my reasons or how I have obtained the information I needed to carry out my mission."

"Are you Melody Ford?"

A gargled laugh escaped the stranger's putrid lips. "Mr. Stone, that is laughable. You really disappoint me."

"Then, where is Melody?" Max was calmer.

"Ah, Melody. Where indeed?"

240

"Did you kill her?"

"Of course I did, Mr. Stone. And I took her reproductive organs to add to my collection, just like I did with Misty, Kaliana, and Anastasia."

"Where is Melody?" Max asked again.

"You know, Mr. Stone, Leah's ovaries will be my most prized trophy."

"I will put a bullet through your brain before you touch my wife." Max's said through gritted teeth. "Now, where is Melody?"

"Mr. Stone, you have persuaded me. Since this is so difficult for you, I will toss you a bone. You will find Mclody's body at the park closest to your home."

Chapter 41

Leah looked at the clock and it read 3:15. She went to Doug's station and asked him if he was ready to go. He was.

She bundled up, told Freda bye and that she would see her tomorrow. Surprisingly, so did Doug.

The two made their way toward the front of the building, out the door, and to Leah's car. She climbed in the driver seat, he got in the passenger side, and she started her car. It took a few minutes for the defroster to erase the thin film of frost that had collected on her windshield. Soon, she put it in drive and they were on their way.

He had told her the address of the repair shop and she pointed the car south. For a few minutes, it was quite uncomfortable for Leah. She never thought that Doug Brewer would be riding in her car. She despised him. Yet, here he was big as life, sitting right beside her in her own car. Most of the time, her blood would boil when she had to deal with him and his insubordination. Today, however, he had actually infused some serious thought into one of her conversations. He, of all people, actually showed hurt over young girls being needlessly killed. After a short while, he broke the uncomfortable silence and engaged conversation with her.

"You know earlier you were talking about those girls being killed?"

"Yes, but I thought you didn't want to talk about that," she said with a reassuring smile. "You made that very clear today." She was still unsure if he was being serious or if she should drop her guard.

"Well, yes, I did, but I was thinking about that very topic and it occurred to me."

"What occurred to you, Doug?" she asked with interest.

"Someone out there doesn't like what we do for a living," he stated.

"What do you mean?"

"Those two girls," he stated with affliction, "were in the Embryonic Stem Cell research program at school, were they not?"

She nodded.

"They were learning to do what we do?" he confirmed.

Again, she nodded.

"They care, Miss Stone. These girls cared about our research and wanted to help people," he said with feeling. "They even talked to you at your seminar about donating eggs, did they not?" he asked.

She nodded again.

"They were the stars of the future in our industry, so to speak," he said. "Somebody out there really hates our line of work. The killer is probably someone who is against the research we do." He paused for a moment and added, "Probably some wacko nut job, bible thumping hypocrite, who believes that only God should have such power."

They rode in silence for a moment as she pondered his thoughts.

"And," he added, "the way these poor girls were killed." He shook his head. "It was almost ritualistic, don't you agree?"

She didn't respond.

"I mean," he added, "anchoring them to the ground like that," he said through a choked voice, "and cutting open their abdomens and taking their female parts and all," he continued to shake his head. "And the note," he paused, "had to be someone dead set against our research efforts."

She thought about his statement. There could be some merit in that. She wondered if her husband had come up with the same conclusion. It did make sense to her. Why would only girls that were in the Biology field at the campus be the target of such a thing? More importantly, they were in the Embryonic Stem Cell program. Deeper yet, these girls attended her seminar and had approached her about donating eggs. They were, wait, how the hell did he know these girls had been to her seminar? How did he know these girls spoke to her about donating eggs? Her files were confidential. Had he overheard her say something to Freda about it? It was possible, but doubtful. He couldn't have heard her conversation with Max a few hours ago. She was alone in her office.

The papers wouldn't have offered any information. The press didn't know. The only thing the paper mentioned was two college students killed. Hell, the paper still hasn't even released the name of the second girl. Wait a minute, there was never any mention of how the girls were killed. The paper did mention that it seemed like a gang or ritual killing but there was never any mention of anchoring them down or the taking of internal body parts. And the note? What note? The paper never, hell, Max never said anything to her about a note!

"What note?" she asked him.

"You know," he motioned with his hand, "the note the killer left behind saying how he needed them more than she did," he said, trying to convince her.

"There was never any mention of any note." she said loudly. "There was never any mention of incisions or the taking of body parts!" She was almost screaming now.

In an instant, a syringe appeared in his hand and he thrust it into her right thigh.

Leah's eyes looked grave as she saw the needle sink into her tender flesh. She tried to protest, but her mouth had turned dry as dust and a lump the size of a fist welled up in her throat.

"No," he said seductively, "I suppose it didn't," he laughed, "but I have just such a note reserved for you, Miss Stone," his deep voice turned satanic.

She felt a rush of heat throughout her body as the drug began to course through her. She felt tired and dizzy.

"Leah, before you drift off into slumber," his sandpapered voice said, "you will pull this car over on your own if you want to save your kids and husband from the same fate you will have. If I have to yank the wheel and stop the car, they die!"

She was barely coherent. She figured she was going to die anyway and thought briefly about mashing the accelerator in hopes of killing them both. Perhaps she could save her family. There was the hope, though, that her husband would find her in time. After all, he was one of the best detectives around. He would eventually figure it out, wouldn't he? She thought about his demand. His word was no good. He could still try to kill her family too, if he wanted. Should she try to kill him, and probably herself in the process or take the chance that she was the one he was really after? Should she pull over willingly? Yes, she would meet his demand.

She felt the darkness pulling at her and her speed slowed. The lines on the road were blurry. She managed to steer the car into the nearest parking lot and put the car in park. Then she slumped, unconscious.

Chapter 42

There was only one place Melody Ford's body could be. It had to be Lawrence Park.

Max and John raced the car across town as John phoned Terry Green. He said he would get all the proper people rounded up and head that way.

The two arrived at the park. No one was there. Lawrence Park was mostly wide open. There were a few trees here and there, but not very secluded. It was nothing in comparison to the other parks where the victims had been found. There weren't a lot of places to hide a body and there wasn't any water. One could pretty much scan the entire park, except for a small tree area near the back. A quick glance netted nothing so Max and John raced toward the small stand of trees near the back of the park.

There she was, Melody Ford. She was anchored to the ground, just like the other girls. Her abdomen had been cut down both sides. Max knew what that meant. Her jeans, like the others, had been cut from her body and tossed to the side, as was her shirt. Her bra was untouched and still in place. The note was safety pinned to her navel.

The frigid air became visible with each exhale of Max's breath. John turned to greet Terry and a host of uniformed officers as Max reached down to retrieve the note. He unfolded it and began to read. His lake blue eyes allowed a hot lava tear to race down his cheek. They dimmed and turned gray.

"What is it, Max?" John asked with concern.

His lips trembled and he could barely speak the words, "He's got Leah."

John snatched the note from his hand and read it:

> *Detective Stone,*
> *You have, no doubt, found young Melody Ford.*
> *Now that you have found her, you should know*
> *I have your precious Leah. She too will feel*
> *the cold steel of my surgical blade. She will*
> *be my most prized trophy. I told you I would*
> *prove you couldn't protect your own wife. I so*
> *hope she doesn't disappoint.*

John's jaw slammed the ground. How could this be? Leah was one of his friends. His heart sank to his shoes. He quickly asked Terry to take command of the crime scene and he led Max away and back to the car.

Max grabbed his cell phone and dialed Leah's number, but got no answer. He did this five more times with equal results.

"Max," John said as he shook him. "I know it's tough, but we've got to focus. We need to get an A.P.B. out right away. We will find her." John encouraged.

It all made sense to Max; the phone calls, the killings, the, well, everything. For weeks now he had fielded several calls from a mysterious voice that, from the very beginning, told him he would kill his wife to show the world he was not a good detective. That was the voice's exact words. How clever to disguise the whole plot in such a way. The whole time Max's attention was diverted with the killing of young women who just happen to be following the same career path as Leah. Max was sure the killer had to be someone against Stem Cell research. The pattern fit such a profile. Hell, even targeting Leah, the pattern fit the profile.

Another tear raced down his cheek as Tank placed him in the passenger seat. How could he have been so stupid? How could he have not seen this coming? Doubts of his ability began to creep into his mind.

"Damn it Max!" Tank shouted at him. "I need you to come back to me buddy," he pleaded. "We may not have much time! I need you to be the super detective that we both know you are." Tank turned to his hurting friend. "Now, if it were anyone else but your wife, and you had as many facts in front of you as you now have what would you do?"

Max thought for moment and shook the cobwebs from his brain. He replayed all the events that brought them to this point. He rubbed his temples, cranked up the blues station on the radio, and began to think.

Moments later, his deep saddened eyes turned slate gray. A furrow placed itself on his forehead and his brows narrowed until his slate gray eyes were mere slits. Stoney was back. He turned down the radio and turned to Tank.

"This son-of-a-bitch done messed with the wrong mother-fucker!" he proclaimed.

"That's my buddy," John said. "What's the game plan?"

Max retrieved his phone and called Leah's office and got no answer. He opted out of the voice mail option and pressed zero and was sent to the operator. When she came on the line, Max asked to speak to anyone in the department and was sent to Freda Lyle.

"Freda? Max Stone. Where is Leah?"

"She left here about an hour ago."

"Where did she go?" Max demanded.

"Oh yes," she replied. "She went to take a colleague to pick up his car from the repair shop."

"Who?"

"Doug Brewer. Why?"

He and hung up without answering.

"That prick Doug Brewer is the killer," Max said. "She's had trouble with him."

"Who, and how, uh..." he was confused.

"You remember," Max gestured, "that dick of a man that she works with."

"Oh," a light bulb went on, "the one she's always complaining about that is always giving her a hard time."

"That's the one," Max said. "She took him to go get his car."

"Well, that doesn't make him a killer," Tank stated. "But, it does make him primary suspect number one."

Max thought for a moment. He couldn't fail now. He had to keep his head right.

"Ok, Stoney," John asked. "Where do we start?"

"Way ahead of you," Max replied as he whipped out his phone again.

John sat and listened intently as Max spoke into the phone.

He sounded official as he began telling the listener on the phone who he was and that it was a police emergency. He gave them Leah's cell number and told them he needed a location on that phone. He sat in silence as he was put on hold.

"Who you talking to?" John asked.

"The wireless phone company," he explained. "I'm going to have them do a triangulation on Leah's phone."

"A what?"

"A triangulation," Max said again. He decided he better elaborate. "The location of a cell phone can be determined by taking a reading from different towers. It is possible to calculate where the signal is coming from by working out the triangle that fits the signal strengths. The third point is the location of the phone, or, at least, reasonably close," he explained.

"How close?" John asked.

"Approximately one-hundred yards or so."

"How the hell do you know that?" John asked in amazement.

"It's not that hard to do. I've done it plenty of times before."

"Don't today's phones have GPS on them? John asked.

"Well, yes, they do, but, depending on your carrier, they may not always be transmitting," he explained. "In some cases, they only transmit a location when a 911 call is made."

"Who knew?" John joked.

"Uh, yes? Ok, thank you," Max said into the phone and then hung up.

"Now let's hope Leah has her cell phone on her," John said. "If she does, the bastard has her at my very house."

Chapter 43

Leah woke to find she had been anchored to the ground. She could not move her arms or her legs. She was trembling from the cold, damp ground. She moved her head to look down her torso and realized she was nearly naked. Her bra was the only thing protecting her from the cold. She looked left and then right. Her clothes and her purse had been placed next to the right side of her waist. Her skin had a bluish tint to it and was blotchy. A chill came over her. She turned her head and heard the frozen ground beneath her crunch, or was it her frozen hair. She wasn't sure.

The haze was clearing from her head. Looking around, she realized she knew this place. Yes! There was the bubbling creek just behind her head and, she turned her head the other direction. Yes! There was the back of her house just off in the distance beyond the trees about fifty yards. This was the little woods behind her house.

She decided she would yell for help and then realized a thick gray layer of duck-tape had been placed across her mouth. She moved her tongue and discovered that some type of cloth had been placed in her mouth as well.

Where was he? Where was that bastard Doug Brewer? She turned again, but didn't see him. Had he brought her here to freeze to death just yards from her back door? Where was Max? Would he figure out she was taken and if so, by whom? Would he save her? A warm tear raced down her cheek and collected in her ear. She was so cold and frightened. She closed her eyes and began to think of happier times and happier places. As quickly as she would think of something happy, thoughts of dying would race back in.

She began to silently pray when she heard his voice.

"Well, Leah," Doug said from behind her.

She couldn't see him. He had positioned himself just beyond the top of her head so there was no way to see him from any angle that she could turn her head.

"I see you have moved to praying," he smirked. "I guess you're about desperate enough now to get on with it."

He moved closer and crawled on his belly next to her. He put his mouth right next to her ear and whispered, "I'm going to take this gag off your mouth. One little scream from you and I will gag you again, go over there to your house, drag your kids out here, and make you watch me kill them." He laughed. "You understand?"

His breath was rancid. Everything about him was rotten. But, she nodded her head in acceptance to his terms.

He pulled off her gag and removed the cloth from inside her mouth.

"Why are you doing this, Doug?" she asked through chattering teeth. "Why did you kill all those innocent girls?"

"Because it was fun," he mocked.

"How did you get their names?" She demanded to know. "I mean it's obvious why you chose the ones you did, but…"

He placed a grimy hand over her mouth.

"You hush now," he said quietly but firmly. "You start getting too loud and I will have to gag you again," he chuckled through his sickening breath. "It was easy getting the list. Breaking into your personal files was easy."

She swallowed hard and tried once again.

"Explain it to me, Doug," she pleaded. "If you're going to kill me, I want to know."

"Aw, now isn't that sweet," he teased her. "You see, Leah, this has all been one big fun game for me. You are on the verge of a major scientific breakthrough in our research. You have created something new for the medical field and it's called Cell Metamorphosis. But you see," he stopped to reflect. "Here's the problem. I've been a scientist for, what, nearly forty years and was considered among the best, at least until you came along."

"And you still are, Doug," she pleaded.

He chuckled at her statement.

"That's funny, Leah," he scoffed. "You, on the other hand, have been a scientist for, oh," he thought for a moment, "maybe seven or eight years. Now, all of a sudden, you are on the verge of a major breakthrough and considered the best there is. Bullshit!" he screamed in her ear.

"So," she wondered, "all of this is driven by jealously?"

He ignored her comment.

"Oh, Leah," he smirked. "Don't you see the beauty in it all? If I kill you, I can retrieve your findings and claim them for my own before the public has been made aware of the discovery. I will be the hero and then I will get all the press and the headlines and the hype." He laughed in his sadistic tone. "I might even get a Nobel Peace Prize," he added with glee.

"Doug, you know you can't get away with this." She stammered through chattering teeth. "If you want the glory, you can have it, but it doesn't have to come to this. You can let me go and I will give you all the glory. I'm not doing it for the glory. I'm doing it for humanity," she pleaded.

"Oh, but I can get away with it, Leah," he whispered in her ear. "That's the beauty of it. The killings, the phone calls to your husband," he paused. "All of it was designed to deceive and mislead. Everyone, including you, was fooled. Everyone believes that it's someone against Stem

256

Cell research when actually, that couldn't be further from the truth." He laughed.

"You called Max?" she asked.

"Oh, yes, several times," he mocked with excitement. "Oh," he looked at her and made a fraudulent sad face, "he didn't tell you?" He shook his head. "I have him believing that I'm just someone that wants to kill his wife to prove that he sucks as a detective." He laughed at her. "By now, he believes that the other killings were just a ruse to throw him off the trail, since these other girls are going to school to do what you do for a living," he paused. "Well, up until now." He laughed again.

He propped himself up on his elbows and pushed himself to a sitting position. He reached for a satchel that had been placed beyond her line of vision above her head and drew out a surgical scalpel.

Leah drew in a quick breath.

"Doug, no," she pleaded. "You don't have to do this. I will do anything you want."

"I knew you wouldn't disappoint me, dear Leah." He moved and swung his leg over her body and positioned himself to sit across her legs. "It is time," he said as his voice deepened and became more graveled.

"I will do anything you want, Doug," she cried. "Please, you don't have to do this!"

For a moment, she thought her pleading changed his mind as he placed the scalpel on the ground beside her. Her heart broke once more as he shoved the washcloth back into her mouth and stuck the duck-tape back on her mouth.

Her eyes struck fear as he picked up the scalpel once again. His eyes were distant, almost possessed.

"Now, Leah," he smiled as the light glinted off the steel. "Shall we begin?"

She watched him as the blade drew closer to her belly. She felt the cold blade sink into her skin and instantly felt warm blood rush to the surface of the cut and trickle onto her abdomen.

He squealed with delight as he began to draw the blade in the arcing curve of his abdominal cavity.

She fought against her restraints. Pain sensors were screaming inside her head. She felt her flesh pull away from itself as she felt the blade begin to slowly cut and mutilate her. She bucked her hips, trying to throw her assailant off of her.

Suddenly, a thunderous cracking shot broke the silence of the air and she felt her captor's blood spray on her face and body. His face showed sudden shock, and he slumped from his position on top of her and fell to the ground. She was in so much pain it took her a moment to register what had happened. She turned to look around. She saw nothing at first, except Doug's dead body lying beside her. His head had been blown half off.

Her eyes began to focus and then she saw him standing at the edge of the tree line. It was Max! Blackberry smoke trickled from the end of his pistol, which was still raised and steady in his right hand. His jaw still clinched and his face stern.

John rushed to Leah from the opposite side. He apologized to her for seeing her "Stoney only" parts as he shed his coat, and placed it over her body. He then tore off his shirt and held it on her open wound. He pulled out his pocket knife and cut her loose, but told her to lie still and hold his shirt firmly on the cut.

Max, rebounded from his own shock, returned Raven to its holster and rushed to his wife. She threw her free arm around him, while holding Tank's shirt on her wound.

Together, they moved her to the house, called an ambulance, and headquarters.

The sound of the ambulance drew closer as Leah's world grew dark.

Chapter 44

It was Christmas morning and The Stone family Christmas tree was done up in their traditional blue lights with silver tinsel. It was a tradition at the Stone's house. Max remembered as a boy, watching his dad decorate the tree. He always did his tree in blue lights and silver tinsel. There was something about the soft glow of blue against the dark green of the tree. Today, Max did his tree the same way his dad did all those years. It was mostly to honor his dad and partly because it brought back a time of youth and innocence.

Max sat and sipped his coffee and allowed his thoughts to return to last night and the annual Christmas Eve party at his brother's house. This too, was an annual tradition started by his dad. The whole family was musically talented and Max enjoyed blowing his blues harmonica and singing with the family. Between himself, his brothers, and nieces and nephews, they had enough for a full band. It was a celebration of family and togetherness. There was always plenty of good food, plenty of good music, and plenty of drinking.

It's been an annual event for over thirty-five years now.

Christmas music quietly filled the air. Luther Vandross was playing on the satellite station on the T.V.

He sat next to Leah, sipping his coffee, and watched the kids, as did she, open their presents with excitement. Even though the children were old enough to know who Santa Claus really was, or not was, there was still a present or two under the tree from old Saint Nick, in addition to the many from mom and dad. There was even a present under the tree from Santa Claus to Max and Leah.

The sound of laughter filled the air as the kids ripped open packages. Police work couldn't be further from his mind right now.

The wonderful aroma of a turkey, baking in the oven, drifted from the kitchen.

Max glanced at Leah as he placed his hand on her thigh. She was curled up in her big fuzzy pink robe. It covered her from nearly head to foot. It covered her bandages around her stomach. She looked at him and smiled, as she placed her hand on top of his, then turned back to watch the kids.

He watched her. Her face beamed with joyfulness. She too, loved Christmas. There was no bigger kid at

Christmas than Leah Stone unless, of course, you included Max in that equation.

He almost lost her. What would have happened had he been even a minute later? A small tear filtered into his eye at that thought. He remembered racing to the house, finding her car in the driveway, but her not home. He remembered the wireless company giving him the location of her phone, but only being accurate to around a hundred yards. Instinct told him to check the small wooded area behind the house. He saw rage when he crept to the edge and saw her anchored down and Doug Brewer on top of her. That blade! Max could feel that blade slicing through her stomach.

He remembered the mysterious voice telling him every murder would get closer and closer to his house. And, they had. Leah was to be his final trophy. And, he had planned on killing her practically in her own back yard.

How clever her, would be, killer was. Almost. In her own neighborhood, hell her own back yard, would be the last place anybody would think to look. He hadn't counted on Max Stone though.

Leah's stitches, one-hundred and forty in all, were healing nicely. She would be ok, physically, except for the eight inch scar she would have down the left side of her abdomen. Mentally, time would tell, but she was in good spirits today.

The sound of ripping paper brought his attention back to home and Christmas. This was the only present he needed.

Leah's cell phone rang and she answered.

"Yes, we're up and ready," she said into the phone. "See you in a couple."

"Tank?" Max asked

She confirmed his question.

Tank and Shawn were as much a part of Max and Leah's family as blood relatives. They would be joining the Stones, as John did every year, for Christmas dinner. Max and John, hell everyone called him Tank, had been friends since they were babies and would be life-long friends, no matter what.

"Wonder why he called you?" Max wondered. "You two got something going on behind my back?" He joked.

"Well, honey, you know," she said, acting guilty.

The kids were finishing up the last of the presents as the doorbell rang.

"Must be them now," Max said as he got up to get the door.

He cheerfully greeted his friend with a huge bear hug, and then kissed his cheek as he pointed up to the mistletoe. This brought huge laughter from all.

"You don't get off that easily," Max said as he grabbed Shawn and hugged her and then gave her a small kiss on the lips.

Tank had made his way past Max and had gone over, with some mistletoe of his own and found Leah.

"Two can play that game, Stoney," he teased Max as he kissed Leah.

"What the hell?" Max questioned as it dawned on him. "You just called like, what, two minutes ago. Were you sitting outside?"

"Yeah, pretty much," Shawn answered for him.

"I've got some presents to bring in," Tank said as he excused himself and went back out into the cold.

"Oh, honey," Leah said to Max.

He turned to her, "Yes?"

"I do have one more present for you," she said playfully. "Well, actually it's from the family."

Max acted like a kid.

"Tank will be bringing it in," she smiled. "I hope you like it."

The door opened and Tank appeared in the doorway. He was holding a black and white puppy. A tear of joy hit Max's eyes. Tank placed the dog on the floor and Max whistled for it. The puppy clumsily ran to him, wagging his small tail.

Max realized it was an Australian Shepherd and he was beautiful.

Max, with puppy in hand, walked over to Leah, hugged and kissed her, thanked her, and told her he loved her.

Yes, Max was happy. It was Christmas, he had his family, he had his friends, and now, he had a dog.

"What should we name him?" Max asked. He sought input from anyone who had a suggestion.

"How about Blarney?" Leah chuckled.

"Blarney Stone?" Max laughed. "How appropriate."

They all laughed.

GREG COLE

www.ingramcontent.com/pod-product-compliance
Lightning Source LLC
Chambersburg PA
CBHW072204170626
46813CB00003B/786